BAIL OUT!

The plane was starting to buck and weave. The cockpit was full of fumes that seared eyes and throat. It was getting very warm.

Sloan asked, "Will she fly straight enough to ditch?"

"No way," Levy said. "She's taken all she can. I'll hold her."

"No," said Casey Wilson. "I've got her."

"Case," McKay said. His throat was dry.

Casey waved a hand. With his inevitable yellow Zeiss shooting glasses and his tour cap, he looked as if he were just taking the old Piper Cub out for a Sunday spin. "I'll be fine." As if to give him the lie, another explosion cracked inside the cargo department.

McKay nodded and ran for the hatch. He braced and threw himself out of the plane with all his strength, hoping like hell to clear the props.

He tucked himself into a ball as the wind hit him. He felt the awful tug of suction from the whirling, curved black blades. And then he was clear, tumbling over and over.

Above him he heard another explosion.

D1563976

THE GUARDIANS
DEATH FROM ABOVE

RICHARD AUSTIN

JOVE BOOKS, NEW YORK

THE GUARDIANS: DEATH FROM ABOVE

A Jove Book / published by arrangement with
the author

PRINTING HISTORY
Jove edition / March 1990

All rights reserved.
Copyright © 1990 by Jove Publications, Inc.
This book may not be reproduced in whole
or in part, by mimeograph or any other means,
without permission. For information address:
The Berkley Publishing Group,
200 Madison Avenue, New York, New York 10016.

ISBN: 0-515-10267-9

Jove Books are published by The Berkley Publishing Group,
200 Madison Avenue, New York, New York 10016.
The name ''JOVE'' and the ''J'' logo
are trademarks belonging to Jove Publications, Inc.

PRINTED IN THE UNITED STATES OF AMERICA

10 9 8 7 6 5 4 3 2 1

For the Weasel Boys (and Girls)

PROLOGUE ────────────────

With a satisfied belch, Iskander Bey, Protector of Islam, Light of Allah on Earth, Master of the World, lay back on silken cushions looted from the finest store in Barcelona, the fabled and decadent Neiman-Marcus. Beyond the open flap of his pavilion the spring sun shone gloriously on the sands of the Costa Brava and danced high on the Mediterranean chop. After a hard winter the One God was smiling on his faithful.

The infidels of the Federated States of Europe had had it their way last year, after the faithful had burst in upon the continent in a wild jihad firestorm. The man who had once been deputy commander of NATO as Turkish General Hafiz Tülül knew well the terrain he was trying to seize. He had faith that his core of warriors from the mountains and high, windswept plains of Central Asia, Turks and Uzbeks and Azeri, could with the favor of Allah beat both the tough European winter and the soft-bellied nasrani.

But Allah had seen fit to send His chosen greater challenges than anticipated. The minority but sizable Muslim populations

1

of the Balkans had risen in support of the Pan-Turanian mu-jahideen, *even as Iskander Bey had foreseen. The first wave had washed clear to the Carnic Alps on the Austrian border.*

The Slavs had hillmen of their own. The non-Islamic Balkan masses forgot their perpetual feuds to fall on the invaders in a series of savage counterattacks, conventional as well as guerrilla. Much to Iskander's surprise the polyglot FSE army held fast, English, Americans, and Dutch NATO remnants fighting warily but effectively alongside erstwhile Warsaw Pact soldiers, East Germans with West Germans, French beside formerly neutral Swiss and Austrians. Not even the vengeful fervor of long repressed Muslim populations in Albania, Bulgaria, and Bosnia had sufficed to keep the supply lines from Turkey open.

The mutually assured thermonuclear destruction of the twin Great Satans, the U.S. and the U.S.S.R., had hit Islamic fundamentalists like a jolt of crack. The Iranians had never managed to overcome the hostility ethnic Arabs felt toward them enough to spread their own revolutionary brand of that good old jihad religion, and hadn't helped by fighting a brutal, endless war against their Arabic neighbors in Iraq. When the first emissaries of the pan-Turanian crusade began arriving in Arabic countries, before the firestorms had even burned out in Washington, Moscow, and Beijing, a lot of people found the memory of the past glories of the Ottoman Empire a lot more compelling than the memory of how bitterly their great-grandfathers had fought to escape it. Arab and North African hordes leavened with Turkish cadre had swept ashore from small boats at dozens of points along the Mediterranean coast of Europe as the Central Asian thrust crashed into Austria.

But the Syrians and Iraqis and Libyans and Egyptians bringing the true faith to the ancient stronghold of the enemy were mostly warm-weather types. And winter had come harsh to Europe last year.

The Faithful had met many setbacks. They had been beaten back from Austria and Hungary, and the mujahideen *had scarcely grabbed Macedonia from Yugoslavia when a rebellion backed by the hateful Greeks had grabbed it away from them. Cold and disease as much as FSE arms had routed the holy strugglers from France.*

But the crusade was going well in an Italy racked by strikes and civil war, and the Mediterranean coast of Spain remained firmly in Muslim hands from Gibraltar to the Pyrenees. And the year, as the benevolent Allah saw fit, was turning warm again.

A breeze bowed in the walls of the tent. The flap stirred and a woman walked in, golden-haired, golden-limbed, and nude. She smiled, shyly but with a hint of provocation, then settled behind the Bey and began to massage his shoulders. Her fingers, sun-warmed and strong, dug with gentle insistence through a thick padding of fat to the muscles beneath, which were knotted with the tensions of grave responsibility to God and His faithful.

He sighed and settled back, closing his eyes on the sight of a half dozen more long-limbed and naked Frankish women sunbathing on the sand. Messiah-hood had done well by the former General Tülül. It had not hurt his appeal to Sunni Muslims, traditionally wary of, if not actively hostile to, his Shiite sect, that he preached that all strugglers in the holy cause might enjoy on the Earth the pleasures the Koran promised them in Paradise—a pitch unabashedly borrowed from Iskander Bey's predecessor as a champion of Shi'a, Hasan-i-Sabah, the Old Man of the Mountains who had founded the Order of Assassins.

Turkish music skirled on the gentle sea breeze. His nostrils filled with the musky scent of the German woman—a film actress whose luck at being on vacation when the balloon went up hadn't turned out to be as good as she thought—who was massaging him. He felt desire stirring around somewhere beyond the vast mound of his belly. For now it was sweeter to deny himself, to let anticipation grow. As soon as the sun set, he would leave Arenys de Mar for the short journey back to his Barcelona headquarters for the last staff meeting before the spring offensive began in earnest. It would require a debauch to put him in a properly relaxed frame of mind. Perhaps when the need had had longer to build, he would have those twin French fashion models with the long chestnut hair brought in, and let Uschi suck him while they played with each other.

In the distance he heard screams.

For a moment he floated in erotic reverie, imagining himself sliding his hands down the smooth curved cheeks of Antoinette's rump while her sister's lips and tongue made moist devouring sounds below. The vision dissipated before he could plunge himself inside. He frowned.

What is that screaming? I've ordered no executions, *he thought petulantly.* Perhaps I should amend that oversight.

Uschi continued to knead his neck and shoulders. He waved her away with chubby hands, opened his eyes, and looked out past the flap of the tent.

The sea was boiling.

He struggled to his feet, with the help of the actress and a pair of burly body slaves. He had not been exactly slim since his days as a dashing young tank commander, but his weight had ballooned enormously since he had assumed the mantle of champion of Islam. He staggered out into sunlight, his hairy gut jiggling seismically, threatening to burst silken pajama pants.

At first he thought it was a waterspout; he'd never heard of one appearing under such a cloudless sky, but then he'd never actually seen one in his life.

But no, it was a great pillar of steam piling up into the perfect sky, rushing up from a great roaring hole in the surface of the sea. It was as if an invisible heated sword blade was being plunged into the water half a kilometer offshore.

Was being drawn toward him.

He bellowed for his aides. Tribesmen from his handpicked security battalion were running through the bevy of sunbathers into the surf. Chosen for fanatical personal loyalty rather than sophistication, they were emptying the magazines of their assault rifles at the approaching steam cloud.

The cloud boiled through the surf, and the Chosen of Allah became aware of a roar like continuous thunder. A security guard took light like a flare, with a ripping crack as the ammo in his spare magazines cooked off and the scream of one already dead as superheated air vented from his lungs.

Iskander Bey's houris were fleeing, mouths open in cries of terror he could not hear. His favorite, the Spanish girl he called Yasmin, ran directly toward him, her tanned arms outstretched in supplication.

And then her black hair flared into a brief nimbus, and her beauty blackened, and she fell, a calcined mummy.

Immobilized in horror, Iskander Bey watched as the invisible sword drew a line of incandescent sand toward him with demonic deliberation.

CHAPTER
ONE

A bloated black bat shape swept down out of the stars. Roaring, it slotted itself between parallel lines of flares that burned like magenta reflections of an invisible and unnaturally exact constellation. Tires kissed cracked asphalt with a fat girl's squeal.

Four men stood by the neglected county road as the dark giant passed by, whipping the flames of the refuge campfires behind them. The youngest of them dipped the bill of his Radiators tour cap.

"Not shabby," he said. It was high praise. Or at least the highest praise Lieutenant Kenneth Wilson, highest-scoring American ace since Korea, was going to spare the pilot of a mere cargo plane.

Around the brushwood fires the Vietnamese discussed the landing in a low singsong. Even the children were quiet. The remnants of the blaze that had burned them out of the derelict resort complex they had made their home bled angry orange light into the sky beyond a spur of the Laramie Mountains to the southeast. Some of the younger ones had been born in

America, had not known what it was like to be driven from home before the One-Day War two years before. But the latest tragedy had been sudden and comprehensive enough to affect even the old disaster hands, the ones who had immigrated after the collapse in '75, had been boat people in the late seventies, or had gotten out as the Vietnamese civil war began to heat up again in the early nineties, part of the global overture to the Third World War.

Half a kilometer to their left, the Super Hercules out of Andrews pirouetted with its weird elephantine grace in a flare-marked area where flat, hard-packed soil winged out wide to either side of the road, for the whole world like a hippo ballerina from *Fantasia*. Lieutenant William McKay, formerly of the U.S. Marine Corps and currently head of the elite team called the Guardians, took a burned-down stub of cigar from his lips and tossed it to the ground at his feet.

"Bus is here," he said, grinding the butt out beneath the heel of his combat boot. "Time to boogie."

The C-130 waddled back along the road toward them. The Guardians stooped, slung their personal rucks and weapons. The rear ramp was dropping as the big plane drew alongside them.

"Every time I see a Hercules taxiing in like that," said the tall, athletically built man with the James Garner looks, "I think about that airfield in Pennsylvania."

"It's always a joy having you around, Sloan," McKay said. "Even when we're not in the shit, you can always come up with something to be depressed about."

That airfield in Pennsylvania had been a domestic—which meant illegal—CIA asset where the Guardians were supposed to deliver President Jeffrey MacGregor after they got him out of the D.C. holocaust, for the Company to forward to the supersecret Heartland complex buried beneath the farmlands of Iowa. It turned out to be a trap laid by the renegade Roman faction of the CIA; a minigun-mounted Hercules gunship had been the lid intended to slam down hard on them. Through a combination of luck, skill, and down-home meanness they'd survived, leaving the Herkie a burning wreck on the runway as they cut and ran.

Back then, with the fires of World War III still raging across
half the world, they had at least had the firepower, armor,
and mobility of Mobile One to protect them—though the armor would've been no more help than so much wet Kleenex
if the mobility hadn't kept them out of the Hercules' line of
fire long enough for the firepower to kick in. Now they didn't
even have the dubious advantage of a ten-ton armored car;
the current Mobile One was lying in the middle of a nearby
stream, left for dead when its fuel pump cashed in after bringing them safely from the hell-orange heart of a forest firestorm.

Casey Wilson and Sam Sloan—the mechanically inclined
members of the team, though fourth Guardian Tom Rogers
could probably have helped, too, since he could do anything—had been in the process of repairing it, with a spare
from a cache laid down as part of Project Guardian before
the war, when the call from Washington came through. It said
drop everything and leave *now*. Since the call beat the Herkie
sent from the capital to make pickup by not quite six hours,
they figured Washington meant it. Mobile One was going to
have to lie there a while longer.

The Hercules stopped, or anyway slowed to an almost im-
perceptible crawl. Though the war had been history for almost two years, things still hadn't settled down enough that
you could ever be sure a given stretch of ground wasn't Indian
country. Or it might have been that the flight crew had bad
memories of their own; over the winter a team of Effsee sa-
boteurs had lured another Herkie to flaming doom using stolen Guardian recognition codes, not too many klicks from
here.

A ghostly glow waved insistently from the ramp dropped
like an insect's ovipositor beneath the high tail. As they ran
forward, unconsciously bending into the blast of the curved
graphite-epoxy props, the figure of a crew chief gesturing at
them with a green shake-'em-up bioluminescent light baton
resolved out of the night.

The Herkie was moving faster than it looked from the side
of the road. They had to jog to catch up. McKay in the lead,
they jumped one by one onto the vibrating ramp.

The chief was squinting carefully at them. "Yep. You're the Guardians, all right." He had a grasshopper-leg mike curving in front of his face from the headset clamped over his silver-dyed Mohawk, but his words weren't repeated in the tiny bone-conduction speakers taped behind their ears; the statement all but disappeared into the humming, rattling roar of the big machine.

"And you're Tide Camp," McKay returned, in his best Parris Island DI bellow, which even the engine howl couldn't drown out.

The chief nodded and grinned.

"Surprised to see old Maggie's let you keep the Look."

The chief's face fisted. "She don't tell Soong how it goes."

"Say there, McKay," Sam Sloan yelled in his ear, "you planning on entering the aircraft, or are we going to make the whole flight out here on the promenade deck?"

Inside, they walked through the round, cathedral emptiness of the cargo bay, dimly lit by safety lights, as the engine whine rose in pitch and the aircraft gathered speed. Sloan and Rogers flaked off to claim a share of the rack space offered by the blue cargo pads strewn around. McKay and Casey Wilson secured their rucks and long-arms, Casey his heavy-barreled sniper's rifle, and McKay his supposedly lightweight Maremont M-60E3 machine gun. Then they headed on into the two-story flight deck, Case because you couldn't keep him once he got on an airplane and McKay because he was too keyed-up for sleep.

Old campaigner that he was, he could usually zone off anywhere, anywhen. But the nocturnal summons had him going; nothing quite like this had come down since the war. He couldn't keep his mind off it. Maybe that was what they called the burden of command.

Royal pain in the ass of command was more like it.

The Herkie was just sweeping through a turn at the other end of the klick and a half of level road marked by flares, to turn the blunt snout into the wind. McKay grinned out at the stars and magenta flares wheeling by outside, striking jewel sparks off the Plexiglas canopy.

"Just like a Disneyland ride," he said.

The pilot gave him a brief smile and nodded. He was a tightly wound black man with short hair who showed none of the distinctive Tide Camp Look, which tended to be *Apocalypse Now* by way of *Road Warrior*.

"I'm Lieutenant Carey," he said. "Welcome aboard."

Somebody leaned down and tapped McKay's shoulder as Carey and his copilot turned their attention to the Hercules' lumbering takeoff run. This one did have the Camper Look to him, if the chain of tiny plastic skulls dangling from one ear was any indication.

"I'm Levy. Systems engineer. Boys wanna find a place to sit until we get this hog aloft?"

McKay looked at Casey, who was practically vibrating with excitement at being back in a cockpit, even if he didn't actually have his hands on anything—kind of like a sailor in a titty bar after six weeks at sea, he thought. *Boy's getting pathological about wanting to fly.*

"Naw," he said. "We'll stand and watch. We're old hands at this."

The engineer shook his head in sham disapproval. "Federal regulations forbid standing in the aisles during takeoff."

"Screw federal regulations."

"I can see you boys ain't gonna fit too well into modern-day Washington," said the navigator from his elevated seat next to Levy.

McKay grunted.

One thing about the Hercules that had always impressed him was how short a takeoff roll it took to get one's bulk into the air. This one was a so-called Super Herkie, retrofit before the war with uprated engines and these weird-looking high-tech propellers, and it just seemed to jump into the crisp Wyoming air like a sounding whale.

"That's it," the copilot said. "The *Winged Pig* is officially airborne once again. Christ knows how she does it."

"Nick doesn't believe in powered flight," Levy explained.

Lieutenant Carey put the C-130 into a slow portside climbing turn. Levy finished off the introductions: gigantic black-bearded Nick Nicolaitis, copilot, and Turley Stubbs, a skinny son of a bitch with a crooked Appalachian grin and Tide Camp two-tone hair. Carey's first name was Lynn. Levy's was Mike.

McKay watched out the side panels as the little camp of refugees passed by beneath, human circles radiating from the fires like petals of a flower. Nobody seemed to be waving or making any kind of a fuss. They were just down there enduring—as they had, as they would.

In their own backhanded way the flight crew quickly made it apparent that they were impressed to have the famous—or infamous, if you asked, say, Maggie Connoly or former boy-wonder televangelist Nathan Bedford Forrest Smith, now sole owner and proprietor of the state of Oklahoma and environs—Guardians for cargo. They were especially taken with Casey, of course. He was the most famous American combat pilot of their lifetime. Having him aboard was like a garage band discovering Eddie van Halen in the audience for their high-school homecoming gig.

Nick Nicolaitis duly surrendered his seat to Case, proving to be even more huge than he looked sitting down, and went aft to the crew galley to get coffee. Turley rolled back into the upper bunk to make room for McKay to sit.

"Don't need me," he explained. "Ol' Lynn knows how to find D.C. And if he don't, what's the loss? Hear tell Bermuda's nice this time of year."

"So what's the word?" McKay asked Levy as he settled his own bulk in the navigator's chair. "Why the Federal Express treatment?"

Levy showed his teeth and shook his head. He wore his heavy black hair in dreadlocks, which McKay found a little alarming even though he knew what Tide Campers were like—pretty hard-core, as a matter of fact. The military had sure changed since the war.

"We're just shippers and handlers. You know that. They tell us less than you."

"Less and less all the time," said Nick, handing up a couple of mugs of microwave-heated coffee.

"Y'all hear the latest news?" Turley asked. "Don't know if it's got anything to do with you—"

"But it's a good bet," Levy concluded. "I shall now perform a frequency scan. God, isn't science wonderful?"

McKay sipped his coffee. Up front, Carey had turned the con over to Casey, or whatever the hell you called it, and was paying rapt attention as Case brought the bird to altitude. *Gimme a break,* McKay thought, *I could climb this son of a bitch.* And it was true; Guardians training, at Major Crenna's secret camp in the Arizona desert, had been nothing if not comprehensive. Not that anybody's bright twelve-year-old daughter couldn't learn to just *climb* one of the things. *Hero worship's a terrible thing.*

"Got it," Levy announced. "Must be a hot item."

"Tell me it ain't on KFSG," Turley moaned.

"Of course it is, little brother."

McKay winced. KFSG was the Okie City station, broadcasting with a great-big-motherwatt of power to guarantee that down-home tooth-filling and bedspring kind of reception. The FSG stood for Forrest Smith Gospel.

". . . amid continuing reports of the death yesterday morning of jihad leader Hafiz Tülül, generally known as Iskander Bey. A spokeswoman for Chairman Yevgeny Maximov of the Federated States of Europe declined comment on the rumors. However, indications are that a new FSE counteroffensive in southern France is meeting 'confused and demoralized' resistance, in the words of one FSE divisional commander near Nice. . . ."

McKay reached to his breast pocket and woke up his communicator. "Yo, Tom, Sloan," he said, speaking in a normal tone of voice, though all he had to do was subvocalize for the benefit of the tiny mike taped over his larynx. "Hustle on up here. We got something going down."

They materialized, Sloan blinking and looking owlish—Annapolis men knew a little bit about snatching sleep when the opportunity arose themselves. Unfortunately the KFSG newscaster had little of real substance: rumors of some kind of explosion at Iskander Bey's camp in Catalonia, uproar in areas held by the Pan-Turanians, some kind of FSE thrust that sounded a little too comprehensive to be just an extemporaneous reaction to an unexpected opportunity.

"Maybe Maggie's decided to send you to help out the Pan-Turanians now that Iskander's gone," Levy suggested. "She's real into that Realpolitik crap."

" 'The enemy of mine enemy must be my friend,' " Nicolaitis intoned. "Unless, of course, he hates my ass."

"You think this has something to do with why we got called back so suddenly?" Casey asked.

"It could simply be coincidence," Sloan said.

"Yeah," McKay said. "And pigs could fl— I mean, we might be going back to meet the Easter Bunny too."

CHAPTER
TWO ─────────────────

You're supposed to cooperate with the self-proclaimed authorities as far as possible, Toni told herself. *Just keep that in mind.* She leaned against the *Porkchop Express*'s front grille and crossed her arms.

There were five of them. Two were snooping around her trailer, which had been painted a nonreflective buff to minimize the attention it called to itself—not that the snorting of the tractor's big diesel was all that subtle, but after the holocaust you took every advantage you could get. Just like in the movies.

Two more stood conspicuously nearby, admiring the way the waves came into the beach a few hundred meters from the coast road. They weren't watching her, they made clear, but their hands never strayed far from the bulky Glock autopistols in their hip holsters. The last man stood beside their vehicle, a green-painted Brazilian carryall with a big silver methane tank crammed uncomfortably in back, which had whipped a *U* and come to rest facing the *Express*. He had one foot up inside the open driver's door and one resting on the road. The bright early-morning sun of what had been southwestern Oregon turned the lenses of his sunglasses to blank quicksilver pools, staring at her like insect eyes.

The sun stung the points of her shoulders where the weight of her bombardier's jacket rested. The blacktop was uneven beneath her boot soles, buckled by almost two years of neglect. She kept her arms folded tightly over her chest, not because she was cold—though there was still a salt-edged spring chill in the air, despite the sun's aggressive glare—but because she was getting pissed off.

Bad enough that her mission had been aborted. The California Survivors' Cooperative was the big engine of economic recovery in what had been the wealthiest state of the union. Two wars, one the receiving end of a remote-control thermonuclear barrage by the Soviets, the other the up-close-and-personal fight with the Federated States of Europe army of occupation. Not that the state had been doing all that well before the One-Day War; protectionist legislation had done such a fine job of honing America's competitive edge that fifteen percent of the state's work force couldn't find a job, and that was five percent better than the national average of twenty.

But a lot of survivors under the guidance of an Israeli-born economist and former tank-brigade commander had worked their butts off to make it possible for themselves and others to live more than a sunken-eyed, hollow-cheeked *The Day After* subsistence life. Dr. Morgenstern had intended to use this quick run across the Oregon border to a refugee community in the former Siskiyou National Forest to establish the right of free trade among catastrophe's children.

It was a high-risk zone, even though the competing "progressive" governments of the state both claimed to welcome commerce. The Survivors' Coop intended to trade the trailer load of alcohol-burning donkey engines, pharmaceuticals, and high-yield seeds from the New Eden labs to the people, not add it to the booty the urban-elite soviets had expropriated from "hoarders." There were those who said it was too high-risk for a 165-centimeter woman—especially after her would-be partner got liquored up and went missing.

The people who said that didn't know Toni.

She would have pulled it off, too. But their would-be trade partners had developed a sudden case of cold feet. One or another of the state's mustang governments had developed a little too paternal an interest in the proceedings. The Oregon retreaters were a bunch of wimps, anyway. Otherwise they never would have let jerk-offs like that boss them around.

The fifth man started back over from the patrol vehicle. Toni straightened up and tossed her head, flipping the long black braid back over her shoulder. He walked to her, frowning down at the notebook computer in his hand.

"Lee, Antoinette," he read. "Is that correct?"

That's Lieutenant Commander Lee to you, asswhite, she wanted to say. But those days were gone forever, as the song said.

"That's right," she said, keeping her voice as level as the ribbon of highway stretching north and south.

So far they were playing this straight. When the carryall had pulled alongside her semi, she'd thought she'd been shopped and considered running it off the road. Recalling Morgenstern's orders, she'd eaten her misgivings and decided to go along for the time being. She wasn't doing anything illegal, after all. The fact that there were five occupants in the vehicle might not mean a hell of a lot; Portland—more likely Eugene—had learned long since that if it sent its watchdogs of socialist modernism out singly or in pairs, it was unlikely to get them back.

So maybe she was going to get away clear. So maybe she was also going to be able to fly under her own power.

The man with the computer was dressed in the same sort of rough-and-ready outdoorsy rig as the rest, jeans and hiking boots and blue work shirt with the sleeves rolled up to just shy of the elbow in his case. He was very tall. The sun turned the hairs on his forearms to gold.

His four good men and true had the scrubbed, well-packed look of fraternity jocks: White Rats, one of her civilian instructors used to call them. The leader of the pack was more your sunburned cagey Edward Abbey redneck type. All found they were your typical Northwest coast eco-leftist genetic mix:

white boys who thought—for the very best progressive and environmentally conscious reasons—that there were altogether too many people in the world who looked like *her*.

He raised his eyes from his screen, looked into her eyes for a moment, or at least in their general direction. Toni faced him squarely, in spite of the fact that he must have been a foot taller than she was. She did not intimidate well, height or mirror shades notwithstanding.

His glance trailed past her. She resisted the impulse to follow his gaze. He nodded, a little too overtly catching a signal from one of his squaddies. Then he looked at her and shook his head.

"Drug running," he said. "Not a good thing, Ms. Lee."

Strong hands grabbed her arms as the two ocean watchers suddenly closed in to either side. She stared at him.

"What the fuck are you talking about?" She didn't bother to fight the double grip.

Something flashed in her peripheral vision. Her preconscious early-warning system IDed it as nonthreatening, in time for her trip-wire reflexes to keep her from flinching. She'd be damned if she was going to lose face in front of a bunch of yoo-hoos like these.

Mirror Shades held up the vial he'd fielded. "This is what I'm talking about."

"That's insulin. There's nothing wrong with that. Be careful with it; it's supposed to be kept refrigerated."

"It's insulin." He nodded. He was playing out a little script with her. The son of a bitch. "Nothing wrong with that, little lady, just like you say. But what *kind* of insulin—that's the problem."

"What do you mean, what *kind* of insulin? It's insulin."

He smirked. He had a dusty, freckle-sprinkled look to him. Sure enough: your textbook case of protracted *Brave Cowboy* adolescence.

"Wrong. According to the label, it's insulin produced by gene-tailored organisms. That's what we call a crime against nature in these parts, Ms. Lee."

"I thought fucking sheep was what you called a crime

against nature. Of course, you probably call *that* standard operating procedure.''

''I suspect you're attempting to smuggle in other unnatural substances as well,'' he said, ignoring the gig. ''We hoped that the means to carry on such evil work had been destroyed by the war. But it seems to have taken the good and left the bad.''

Toni could agree with that last statement, at least where certain residents of the erstwhile state of Oregon were concerned. Dr. Jake—Morgenstern—had a lecture on the subject of why, simply because a war had smashed civilization across a good portion of the globe, everybody wasn't putting on hockey pads and Mohawks and reverting to feudalism or even hunting and gathering, that life-style everybody writes so glowingly of and nobody chooses. Not all the scientists and engineers died, and neither did a lot of other people smart and literate enough to make use of what had been written down about the enormous complex of technology that had sustained the earlier world. For that matter, not all the cultures of recombinant DNA wonders that had been revolutionizing medicine—like the gene-tailored *E. coli* that made insulin—had been wiped out, either.

Somehow she didn't feel this was the time to rattle off the speech.

''There were people this side of the line who needed it,'' she said, grateful for the harsh discipline of peer pressure that had taught her to keep voice and manner even in all circumstances. When she was a little girl, she'd been prone to burst into tears when she got mad, leading people to the erroneous conclusion that she was just a helpless creature who couldn't do anything but cry. That would be just too fucking much. . . .

''They were wrong, weren't they?'' *Big* smile. ''People don't need technology like that. And if they reckon they do, well, I reckon Mother Earth doesn't exactly need them.''

'' 'This ain't rock and roll, it's genocide,' '' Toni quoted.

Gingersnap eyebrows creased up over blankeyed shades. ''What?''

''Where'd you leave your hood and sheet?''

He growled. The White Rat hanging on her right arm jerked

open her leather jacket. He was the smaller of the two, for what that was worth. All these jerks towered over her.

She glowered at the leader, figuring his helper was going for her .357 Dan Wesson snubby in its shoulder holster snugged in her left armpit. Instead his hand closed over her right tit.

Right. The limits of peaceful cooperation had just been passed at Warp Factor Nine. If Dr. J tried to bitch her off, he could sit on an RPG and spin. She kneed the Rat in the nads.

He doubled over her with that familiar frog-gulp noise. She wheeled into him, letting his weight fall at the juncture of his buddy's hand and her arm. His own grip had kind of slacked somehow.

Redneck One was smirking at her past the boy's bulk. *Let the little chink cunt fight. Just makes it better.* She could just about read his ostensible mind.

Like any real macho man, the juvenile cop was wearing his holster unsnapped. Toni twisted her right hand, snaked out his Glock, and put two 9-mm rounds through the front of the boss man's blue Sears proletarian shirt, clipping the plastic third button at eleven and three o'clock, about four centimeters above the navel.

Rat One was still clutching his bunnies. Rat Two was still clinging gamely to Toni and bearing most of the weight of his buddy. His young face was opening wide in sitcom-school-of-acting panic as the realization grew that his gun arm was all tied up and no place to go. Toni swung her stolen piece to bear. . . .

White sparks fired through her brain from the mastoid process behind her left ear. Whether he was just flailing in blind agony, or whether he actually had the presence of mind to do it deliberately, the nut-kicked Rat had put his elbow into the side of her head. She didn't go out; usually you don't, unless your skull goes *crunch*. But reality did kind of wander out of focus.

When she got things sorted out, she was down on the packed gravel-metaled roadside on ass and elbows. Mirror Shades was gurgling and groaning somewhere nearby. Rat

One was nowhere to be seen. Neither was his Glock. The two patrolmen who'd been snooping around her truck were yelling somewhere in the background.

Toni was looking up between her knees at blond, husky Rat Two, who was grinning down at her. There was even more nastiness in that grin than there'd been before. Nastiness that said he was fixing to pick up where they'd left off, only with a few more embellishments now.

He bent for her, reaching, purplish blue lips skinned back from teeth like white cinder blocks. Toni got hold of wood grips custom-carved by the Hogue brothers to fit her small hands, pulled out her .357, stuck it up between the two of them, and pulled one off.

It wasn't an elegant shot, but then she was in a hurry. The semijacketed hollow point splashed against the blond Rat's right cheekbone and blew out that side of his face. He went away.

She rolled. It was a good move. One of the Rats in her backfield had been carrying a nasty little black CAR-15 slung, and he'd popped a three-round burst from behind the *Express*'s trailer.

Needlepoint 5.56 bullets kicked up gravel where she'd lain with a singing, pinging rattle. She was already out of that bad guy's field of vision, chin resting on pigtail just under the tractor's front bumper.

Away off at the far end of the rig, there was a grove of four legs in the sunlight. She picked the farthest inland, lined the wide orange front blade up with the white dots of the rear sight, *squeezed* one off.

The revolver had an underweight frame, another nod to her damn doll-like hands. It didn't eat much of the short, savage recoil. She let it ride up, controlling it as well as you could, double-actioned a second round when the weapon fell level.

The hiking-booted foot flew away in a spray of red, to be replaced by the torso of the CAR-gunner. She held down on him for a fraction of a heartbeat, just long enough to confirm that he'd lost his grip on the submachine gun and was busy writhing and clutching at his shattered shinbone.

The other pair of feet danced a moment, then just vanished. Grinning, she rolled and doubled to cover behind her, realizing at once that the final Rat had jumped straight up and was clinging like a baby opossum to the rear of her trailer to keep her from blowing his pins out from under him.

The two she'd shot first were down but still seemed to be breathing. The Rat she'd given the knee to remained among the missing. There was some scrub growing in the ditch where he'd probably taken cover.

She bounced up. As she darted for the driver's door a bullet gonged into the flat face of the tractor. She yanked open the door and dived inside.

Wishing she had eyestalks like a crab, she poked her head up just far enough to peer over the dash. Instantly the windshield starred, the epicenter twenty centimeters high and left.

"Son of a *bitch*," she said. The fucker she'd kneed hadn't just recovered his breath; he'd recovered his sidearm and was firing her up from his shrub.

But her eyes were better than good, her vision trained to pick a tiny sliver of MiG out of a cloud. She'd spotted the puke.

As of this moment neither could see the other. She hauled the Franchi combat scattergun out of its under-dash brackets and braced its butt plate against the seat back. It was a nasty, late-model piece that looked like a black broom handle with a pistol grip and a heavy box magazine slotted behind it, bullpup style. Her first shot blasted the windshield out in glittering spindrift. The next two rounds sprayed the patrolman's bush with clouds of triple-ought buck.

She dropped the shotgun on the seat. Keeping low, she gunned the big diesel and shifted into gear. She didn't know if she'd hit the bastard or not, but she was willing to bet she'd given him enough to think about for the moment.

Groaning, the semi rolled forward. The Rat she'd shot in the face lay clear of her tires. The leader didn't. Toni made a face at the bump and crunch with wet accompaniment.

Porkchop Express didn't gather speed quickly. But its mass built up momentum real fine. It just sort of nudged the carryall playfully in the snout, buckling its frame and shoving it tail first into the shallow ditch. Then the semi was moving, tires singing on blacktop.

Toni heard a spatter of quick shots. The boy in the bushes was at it again, and from the sound of it, somebody had the CAR-15 in action too.

Her eyes flipped to the rearview. The CAR's original owner was out of it—hard to concentrate when your shin's been turned to scrimshaw toothpicks—but his buddy had recovered the piece and was kneeling to fire after her as if he were on the firing line.

She frowned. The auxiliary fuel tank was pretty well protected, and diesel fuel wasn't as touchy as gasoline, which her predecessors in her chosen profession had named Orange Death for good reason. But the insulin vials were breakable, and that stuff could mean life for some poor fuck.

She saw the other patrolman come out of the bushes and dive into the car. She locked the brakes and relished the way the big machine fought her.

He wasn't too dumb, for a White Rat. His stupid Austrian popgun wasn't going to do her any harm. The radio in the vehicle was a lot more potent weapon right now. If he was out of Eugene, he might just be able to call in air support to interdict her—if you could call a scrubby collection of Air Guard trainers and a pair of ancient Cessna A-37 Dragonflies the DEA had been using to chase dope fliers coming in from Canada "air support."

This could not happen. Because even their miserable, wired-together excuse for an air force could blast the *Express* into something you could have spray-painted red back before the war and gotten a city council to buy for urban public art. And that would be too humiliating an end for the woman who might have been America's first female combat aviator to take.

The *Express* got stopped without jackknifing or doing anything too radical. She pulled another implement out from under the dash, broke it open to check its load. It resembled a fat, single-shot shotgun and was stubbier than was real comfortable for her to handle.

Oh, well. She hadn't needed giant hands to play the HOTAS joystick controls of her F-18 interceptor like a concert pianist. She'd be damned if she'd let more primitive weapons systems get the better of her.

She opened her door. A bullet hit it and went whining off for a stand of trees a couple hundred meters east of the roads.

"Damn," she said. The one son of a bitch had realized you could *aim* a CAR-15, rather than just spew bullets all over everywhere. He was maybe three hundred meters away; might even be able to nail her, if he was a good enough shot. A CAR-15 had a better range than the short barrel seemed to indicate.

That just changed her targeting priorities. She pulled the M-79 to her shoulder, sighted, fired. She had the grenade launcher broken open when she saw the flash, right where she wanted it.

The thud of the explosion reached her while she was leaning inside the cab to fish another high-explosive/dual-purpose grenade out of the glove compartment. When she looked again, the CAR gunner was lying sprawled beside the road.

The carryall was cake. Neither she nor it were even *moving*. The forty mike-mike grenade spiraled right in the front window while the would-be rapist was still trying to get on the horn to the high command.

There were no parachutes.

She took her time recharging her weapons and getting them stowed away again. If the Teeny-Weeny Air Force had scrambled on her she wouldn't get away anyway. But it was liable to be a while before anybody on the ground arrived to investigate the pillar of black smoke from the blazing carryall.

She sent *Porkchop Express* rolling south in a guilty kind of exaltation. It was a dirty kind of fighting, not at all the clean, aloof combat of the air; she had dust-caked drops of something she was sure had to be blood drying on the back of her shifting hand. But it was a release of sorts from the anger and frustration that had been building since the One-Day War.

She was almost *grateful* to the White Rats. And that showed how badly she needed to get back in the sky.

Fat fucking chance.

CHAPTER
THREE ————————————————————

"You're telling us Chairman Max has gotten himself some kind of space laser base?" McKay shook his head. "C'mon, Doc. Tell us another."

Dr. Lee Warren grinned. "Not only does he have a space laser base," he said, "but it's one of *ours*. How do you like that?"

The air-conditioning in the briefing room in the depths of the White House was enough to raise hair on a dead man. A dead *bald* man. McKay took out a cigar, took off the cellophane wrapper with the weird Indonesian writing on it, and stuck it in his mouth.

"Sucks," he said.

Sam Sloan frowned, looking as earnest as a Sunday school student trying to suck up to the teacher. "How is that possible?" he asked. "That implies that America was able to put a fully functional high-energy laser into orbit without anybody becoming aware of it."

"Pretty ridiculous, huh?" Warren was enjoying this. He was in racquetball trim and had a boyish look to him despite graying hair, which he wore long. He stood at the end of the table with a leather-patched gray suede sport coat elbow up on the podium and a Reebok propped on a chair, looking like the kind of ultra-hip professor whose classes were always overbooked and who tended to turn up on the TV when the public needed the inside on what the cutting edge of science was cutting into. In other words, he looked like just what he'd been before the Third World War turned him into just another rock and roll refugee.

"Almost as farfetched as putting a whole secret national emergency command post underneath the state of Iowa without anybody catching on."

The Guardians looked at each other. That was a pretty fair capsule description of Heartland, the bolt hole to which the Guardians had delivered President MacGregor after the One-Day War. Warren knew what he was talking about. He was a participant in the Blueprint for Renewal, a top secret scheme for rebuilding America in the wake of thermonuclear war. Once the Guardians had MacGregor safely emplaced in Heartland, it had been their duty to hunt down as many Blueprint specialists—not just scientists but engineers, administrators, experts of every stripe—and pack them back to the subterranean facility to get down to business. Warren had been one of them.

Casey was rubbing the longish blond hair over one temple with a forefinger. He was stacked sort of sideways in his chair, with one of his lengthy legs draped over the arm.

"Have to be a pretty powerful laser, man," he said. "It'd take a lot of power to drive a coherent beam through the atmosphere and still have enough energy left to make much of an impression on the surface. I mean, if that's, like, really what happened to Iskander Bey."

"Precisely true," said Warren, nodding the way he might to encourage an exceptionally promising undergrad. "It seems likely that such a system would make use of a wavelength to which the air is extremely transparent, such as ultraviolet. That's of course the high-energy end of the spectrum, and producing a beam that hot would draw a lot of power. On the other hand, in space there's never any energy shortage as

long as the sun's still burning; it was mostly political consid-
erations that prevented construction of solar-power satellites
years ago that would have eclipsed even Project Starshine in
ability to produce cheap power.''

Starshine was the code name of a Blueprint fusion-power
generation project hidden in Louisiana's Wolf Bayou. The
Guardians had fought hurricanes, an Effsee expeditionary
force, and a renegade Cuban frigate to reclaim it. What it
mainly needed was a means of tying into a widespread dis-
tribution grid to begin contributing to the rebirth of America.

''This is admittedly outside my area of expertise; I'm a
quantum mechanic, myself,'' the physicist said. ''But it seems
to me that if you tied an orbital solar-power collector to a
laser built around even such high-temperature superconductor
technology as was generally available before the war, you
might be able to produce some pretty impressive effects.''

''How likely is it that something like this really was involved in the disappearance of Iskander Bey?'' Tom Rogers
asked in his eternally soft, almost soothing voice.

''Very high order of probability, Lieutenant. Very high indeed. First of all, the speed of the FSE reaction leads us to
virtually rule out accident, as you've no doubt already concluded. They weren't exactly taken by surprise.''

The Guardians glanced at each other, nodded. Disasters
didn't just *accidentally* happen to enemies of Chairman Max.

''Our first hypothesis as to what had happened was a liquid
propane gas explosion; just such a mishap occurred on the
Catalan coast back in the late seventies or early eighties. That
would be a very expensive means of assassination and could
get you penalized for unnecessary roughness, but it could
also be quite effective. You'll recall that the only real honest-
to-goodness firestorms the One-Day War created in North
America involved LPG release.''

''But you don't think that was it,'' McKay said around his
cigar. His jaw ached with the desire to fire that puppy up.
It'd be a gas, too, if only to get on the fortunately absent
Maggie Connoly's tits—she'd done everything she could to
ban smoking outright in the capital, just like the old days—

but the more important consideration was that his buddies would kill him if he lit that rope in here.

"No. Emergency-band traffic from the Barcelona area is completely inconsistent with an LPG blast. Nobody's reporting any petrochemical smell, and while there've been reports of a flash, those are sparse enough that they probably come from witnesses whose minds supplied that detail after the fact, or people who didn't witness anything at all but want to get in on the act. There was noise, but that's fairly consistently reported as a roaring or continuous thunder, not one big boom. And the effects seem to be localized, instead of blanketing the area the way a liquid propane or other fuel-air explosive blast would. Naturally reports of any kind are pretty thin on the ground; anything that might bear on the actual whereabouts or safety of the Mahdi Iskander has had a lid clamped on it hard."

"Do we know whether Iskander Bey is in fact dead?" Sloan asked.

Warren flipped a hand in the air. "If our analysts have any solid data on that, I'm not tied into the right need-to-know circuit—that's an important principle in Washington these days; you boys might want to keep it in mind. My hunch is they don't know anything more than you do. At this point it's worth the life of anybody in the Pan-Turanian-occupied territories to go out over the air with anything at all pertaining to their Prophet's safety—and I'm not just blowing hyperbole; a security squad machine-gunned a deejay in Santander on the air for offering a prayer for the repose of Iskander's soul. If he's hurt, his loyalists won't want word going out, to prevent somebody else from grabbing at the big chair while he's indisposed, and if he's history, his flunkies are going to want to be sure they've got a firm grip on power before they reveal the fact that he's been recalled to Allah's head office. That make sense?"

The Guardians glanced at Tom Rogers, who was nodding his head. He didn't have beyond a high-school education, but with his vast experience as a U.S. Special Forces cadre man in various pestholes around the world, he had more solid knowledge of real-life politics than the whole faculty of Georgetown University.

"Anyway, that's beyond the scope of this briefing, as the government types would say. The big worry we have is *how* whatever did or did not happen to Iskander did or did not happen. One important clue for us was reports from jihad naval patrol vessels operating nearby and militia units on shore of some kind of disturbance in the water near Iskander's pavilion. It was variously described as a waterspout and a great pillar of steam. Either one could be consonant with a high-energy weapon unloading into the water."

McKay frowned and rubbed the side of his jaw. He'd shaved on board the Herkie just before they dropped rubber at Andrews Air Force Base by the dawn's early light, but he was getting some rasp, which pissed him off. If he was still a DI, he'd make himself drop and give him fifty at the least.

"That sounds to me like they're hunting around for the target," he said. "Whatever happened to pinpoint accuracy?"

Warren grinned. "Same thing that happened during the One-Day War: turned out to be a lot more wishful thinking than anything else. Even with the kind of computer-assisted optics we have in space now, getting a high-resolution image of the surface in real time isn't as easy as you might think. And you have the possibility of atmospheric diffraction of the beam, even if the air is real transparent to the wavelength you're putting out, and finally the fact that unless you're firing from a geosynchronous orbit, which'd be a hell of a long shot, you're shooting at a target moving with the earth's rotation."

"Would they take a chance shooting at a target that important unless they had the tracking solutions worked out?" Sam asked. He'd been gunnery officer on the cruiser *Winston-Salem* when the Libyan missiles hit her in Sidra Gulf. When it came time to sling buzzwords like *tracking solutions* he got real anal-retentive.

The scientist shrugged. "What would they have to lose? If they never got their beams to track right, they'd probably still scare the bejesus out of old Iskander and might even get some of the faithful wondering whether he'd lost his mana, if the One God was starting to poke at him with cosmic flaming swords.''

Sloan made the kind of face he'd made when he bit into a green persimmon as a farm boy in the Ozark foothills of Missouri. "This still strikes me as pretty hypothetical, Doctor.''

Warren pushed out his long lower jaw and nodded. "Yeah. I see your point. No fear; we did not haul you out of scenic Wyoming in the middle of the night just because we didn't happen to catch anybody actually pouring gasoline on Iskander Bey. That waterspout struck one of our bright boys as suggestive, and he ran a search of the satellite database. And he came up with *this*."

What looked like a blank stretch of wall behind Warren lit up with a tech drawing of what at first glimpse looked like a semi-random collection of plumbing.

"Cygnus Earth Orbital Station. Orbital height, three hundred fifty kilometers, inclination seventy degrees. What that means is that, in the fullness of time, it passes over just about every settled hectare of the surface.''

A window in the screen showed Earth rotating inside a thin white ring. The ring turned, coloring the globe white where it passed, until the planet was whited-out roughly from Arctic Circle to Antarctic.

"At 0945 Greenwich Mean Time yesterday, Cygnus was passing directly over the Catalan coastal town of Arenys de Mar, about five kilometers from where Iskander had his pro tem pleasure dome pitched. Or right on the money, as we scientists say.''

Casey looked pained. "That's awfully thin, man. There's, like, some piece of space junk passing over just about anywhere at any given moment.''

"Quite astute, Lieutenant. That reminds me, every time I say *lieutenant*, three sets of ears perk up, and even Lieutenant Commander Sloan starts to look expectant. You ought to talk Jeff into promoting one or two of you, make it easier to keep you sorted out.

". . . but, anyway, if that sounds coincidental to you, try this on for size: we ran a check of the Blueprint database. And Cygnus checked out with a top-priority burn-before-reading secret reference.

"You still think we're talking blue-sky here, gentlemen?"

CHAPTER
FOUR ────────────────────────

Take a picture. Make it a map of America, like you used to have in all those dipshit social studies classes in junior high or middle school or whatever the hell, with little pictures of Important Resources. Factories. Water desalinization plants. Fusion reactors. Dudes with big heads. *That* sort of thing.

Cut your map up with a jigsaw, like a puzzle. Then hide each piece in a different part of the country. Keep a careful list of where every piece goes, because sooner or later a Big Nuclear Hammer is going to come down out of the sky and smash the real U.S. of A. into a million million pieces, and then suddenly your little jigsaw map will become vital to putting the whole thing back together again. For security reasons, keep only one copy; this is not the sort of thing you want to fall into the Wrong Hands, if you know what I mean and I think you do.

Then send your one copy of the all-important master list up in an airplane with the president of the United States when the hammer comes down. And then shoot that puppy's ass down into Quebec.

Then get four sad sacks with glowing military records and no immediate family ties, train 'em up real good, and tell them they're hard-core heroes and their job is to find all those little pieces and put them back together. Call the pieces the Blueprint for Renewal. Call your pigeons the Guardians.

You can even mess around some to make the game more interesting. For example, you can have Québecois separatists turn up with a badly damaged master list and one president, who isn't all he used to be, either, to sell to a nasty invader. Then you can fix things so the Guardians get a line into the bad guys' computer net and find out what *they* know, which still isn't a hell of a lot. . . .

Only a totally crazed sadist would play tricks like that on four such swell guys as the Guardians. Just ask them.

"A space laser base is part of Project Blueprint?" McKay asked in disbelief.

Warren shrugged. "We're not sure. There might be other reasons Cygnus is in our database. There are a lot of high-tech manufacturing techniques that require vacuum or low gee, or both. Needless to say, growing perfect crystals for use in compact supercomputers could be construed as worth including in the Blueprint."

"Would that rate the top secret classification Cygnus has?" Sloan asked.

"You got me there, Commander."

Casey was looking worried. "What happened to the people who were up there, anyway? I always wondered about that."

"All personnel in American satellites were evacuated by shuttle as the land war in Europe heated up, except for a few skeleton crews. They all came down after the balloon went up. The crews of several Soviet satellites seem to've been left high and dry. . . ."

He shrugged again. There was no such thing as a totally self-supporting space station. There wasn't a hell of a lot more to say.

McKay was stabbing a blunt finger into the Formica top of

the long briefing-room table. "There's something funky about this. I mean, I figure this laser deal had to be some kind of SDI thing that they were keeping secret 'cause the funds got cut off—''

"No doubt," Warren said. "Also because the Soviets might get irate if they found out a laser capable of delivering a big burn to the surface was orbiting over their real estate.''

"Yeah. So if we had this BFD laser designed to start picking off ICBMs as they came out of the silo, pump up the kill ratio—maybe even knock down sub-launched missiles, like the old SDI they were talking about couldn't do nothing about . . .''

"Yes?" Warren prompted as McKay's voice trailed off.

"So why the hell weren't the sons of bitches up there knocking down the damn missiles that were landing on our heads?''

"Probably hadn't gotten the beam operational yet, Billy," Tom Rogers said. "We don't know how long the Effsees've had to work on this.''

McKay twisted in his chair to glare at the former Green Beret. "You mean you're taking all this seriously?''

"It all hangs together.''

McKay grunted. He had a respect for Rogers's judgment that approached awe. But still—

"This all seems pretty damn circumstantial to me," he growled.

"As a hypothesis, it answers all the big questions, Lieutenant McKay," Warren said. "Do you have something better to offer?''

"Uh," McKay said. "Um.''

"Which, translated from the original Neanderthal, means no," Sloan said, sliding deeper into his chair.

"I still got problems with believing this crap.''

"I don't," a voice behind them said. They turned around to see the president of the United States of America standing in the door behind them.

Jeffrey MacGregor was young to be a president. Only he wasn't looking it nowadays. From the gray at his temples he might've been a man in his fifties instead of his late thirties or early forties. A very fit man in his fifties but middle-aged nonetheless. He was tall, in that indeterminate zone around six feet, like Casey and Sam. The hair that wasn't gray was dark brown. He wore slacks of one shade of gray and a sweater of another, against the artificial winter down here beneath the White House.

He seated himself at the far end of the table from Warren. "If nothing else, gentlemen, we can't afford to take the chance that it may be true."

"Maybe you're right, sir," McKay said. "But what are we gonna do about it, take it out? I mean, even a low orbit's a hell of a pole vault."

"Taking out a satellite's not that big a deal, Billy," said Casey, who was bored by the prospect of shooting something that couldn't maneuver and couldn't shoot back, and showed it. "All you got to do is fire a cloud of solid debris up into its path, sort of like a charge of buckshot. It goes through a cloud of ball bearings at orbital speeds, it's not going to be good for much."

"All of which presupposes we can *reach* it," Sam Sloan said. "Much as I hate to, I'm forced to agree with our esteemed field leader: space is a long way to jump."

"Maybe orbital capability is a Blueprint asset," Tom Rogers said. "Makes sense. Especially if this laser satellite was part of the Blueprint."

McKay made a face. "Yeah, now that you mention it, Tom, I'll bet you're right." He took the unlit cigar from his mouth and studied it as if wondering if it was loaded. "And what's more, I'll bet our friendly analysis gremlins have confirmed the fact, *but* they still don't have a clue as to where we might lay our hands on our dandy launch capability."

"Very good, McKay," Warren said. "If you could just learn to count higher than ten with your shoes on and your fly still buttoned, I might admit you showed some promise."

"Thanks too damn much."

"The obvious location is California," the president said, ignoring the byplay. He had never stood that much on ceremony—and the Guardians were relieved to see Maggie hadn't nagged him into starting now. "All reports indicate the damage at Canaveral was too great for it to be of any use. Whereas at least some of the Vandenberg launch facilities are known to have survived."

"Vandenberg?" Sloan asked, raising one eyebrow like Mr. Spock about to tell Bones what a major dump-brain he was. "I didn't think the Blueprint incorporated out-and-out military facilities. Especially not ones that made as tempting a target to the Russians as Vandenberg."

"The president didn't say Vandenberg was connected with the Blueprint, Commander," Warren said.

"Dr. Warren's right, Sam," MacGregor said. "Our analysts are following all the leads they can through the fragmentary database we've managed to scrape together, and Dr. Morgenstern's people in California are doing all they can to track down the Blueprint launch facility, if it in fact survived the war. But time, as you might imagine, is pressing. Best you go straight to Vandenberg and see what you can do there, and we'll keep you up-to-date."

"Just one point, Mr. President," Sam said, looking puzzled now. "Maybe I'm missing something. Have we in fact received an ultimatum from Chairman Maximov? Do we know for certain that the Cygnus station has in fact been taken over by the Federated States? We might be overreacting here."

"The thing that started this whole garden party was Chairman Max's biggest rectal itch suddenly vanishing in a puff of greasy smoke," McKay said. "You think maybe the Brazilians got hold of the satellite and decided to french-fry this Scumsack Bey just to show old Yevgeny what swell boys they are?"

"And if Chairman Maximov's got something like *this*, man," Casey said, "you can bet he's going to point it at us sooner or later."

"I see your point," said Sloan.

"So now all we have to do is load up a warhead with a buncha scrap iron and sorta pop it off in front of this space-laser dingus," McKay said. "Piece of cake."

"Not exactly," the president said. He seemed evasive all at once.

"What the president means," Warren said, "is that something like this is maybe a little *valuable* to trash out of hand, unless there's simply no other way to go about it."

"Europe suffered a great deal less damage than we did in the war, gentlemen," MacGregor said. "They have more population and more production and generally better organization, in spite of their problems. Chairman Maximov even has at his disposal a sizable remainder of the American forces committed to Europe for the conventional phase of World War III."

McKay growled. "Don't remind us." His buddies—even Tom—had explained how the boys in Europe had a point, with America shattered under thermonuclear barrage, in signing up with what looked like the one force capable of keeping civilization together. To McKay it was still just plain old-fashioned treason, no matter what kind of word games you played to make believe it was all right.

"The important point," MacGregor continued, "is that the Federated States has a tremendous edge on us. A tool— no, a *weapon*, I have to be honest with myself—as potent as this one seems to be could go a long way to redressing that imbalance."

"So what you're saying," McKay said, tying the other Guardians up in a web of shared glances, "is that you want us to reclaim this damn thing? In outer space?"

MacGregor nodded. "If at all possible, gentlemen. Yes."

"Has the strain finally gotten to you," the round-faced woman with the gray-shot brown hair and wire-rimmed glasses asked from the chair with the high padded back, "or are you truly that stupid, Jeffrey?"

Jeffrey MacGregor sighed. *It's what I have advisers for, after all,* he reminded himself. *To give me their candid appraisals. If I surround myself with nothing but yes-men—or women—then I'm in the same boat as a tyrant like Maximov.*

"I'm taking the course of action I deem best."

Dr. Marguerite Connoly made an irritable gesture with both

hands, like an old-fashioned housewife flapping the front of her apron. "Deeming has exactly never been your strong suit. This sort of lapse shows that."

MacGregor looked at her, feeling his eyelids getting leaden even though it was still the middle of a muggy Washington spring morning. The A/C could disperse the heat gathering in the Oval Office. The compressors ran off emergency generators in the basement that had been converted even before the war to burn methane or alcohol as well as diesel and gasoline, thanks to the survivalist mind-set of MacGregor's predecessor, Wild Bill Lowell. MacGregor preferred to keep it off, at least aboveground, where renovations by work crews from Tide Camp had made it possible to actually open windows again, until it got too much to take in late afternoon. He wasn't sure whether he did it from conviction or to keep Dr. Maggie from ragging him for not living in a manner consonant with the Age of *Drastically* Reduced Expectations.

"What exactly do you find objectionable, Doctor?"

"The involvement of the Guardians, among other things. They are atavistic relics of the kind of thinking that got the world in this mess in the first place. You can't solve real-world problems with guns."

"I don't like to think so, either, Doctor," he said evenly. "But while I still consider myself a liberal, I have to admit that a number of convictions I once held dear haven't proved durable under exposure to the real world."

"Some of us have more courage in our convictions, Jeffrey."

He sealed his mouth for a handful of heartbeats. It wasn't so much that he was afraid of her, though he knew that's what the gossip said, in the rubble-choked alleys and sterile corridors. Her capacity for unpleasantness just tended to intimidate him. Like a lot of people of his epoch, he tended to fear confrontation above everything.

"What's your other objection, Doctor?"

"The risk! It's positively insane! If the Federated States of Europe really possesses a space-laser weapon, anything we attempt is futile. They will have the capability of wiping us out whenever they choose."

"We do have bunkers, even here in Washington. I don't believe even such a device as Dr. Warren and his team posits can reach very far underground. And save your breath—you don't have to tell me how inconvenient and unsuitable it would be to run the country from a subterranean base—not that I didn't do precisely that, from Heartland."

He paused, turning over a paperweight in his fingers. It was a Lucite hemisphere containing a picture of him with a bearded George Lucas. *How times change*, he thought.

"We sent the Guardians on a mission with a far greater downside potential not too many weeks ago," he went on, mildly surprised that Connoly hadn't interrupted. She seemed unusually subdued today. "At that time we had reason to believe that the late Colonel Morrigan had some kind of highly infectious biological agent in his possession. Even the nerve gas he actually had to back up his blackmail could have caused untold casualties, if it had been released over population centers."

"I'm quite *cognizant* of that, Jeffrey," she said, speaking with the sharp but measured cadence of a teacher addressing a brain-disadvantaged student. "But at least at that time we enjoyed the full cooperation of Chairman Maximov and the FSE."

"Because the prospect of a runaway superplague scared the chairman as green as it did us," MacGregor said with an ironic half smile. "Do I detect a note of admiration for the chairman's methods?"

"Not his methods. Nonetheless, the efficiency offered by a more unified system of government is bound to command respect."

" 'Unified system of government.' Hmm. Sounds a lot like a dictatorship."

Connoly pinched her mouth and shook her head as if shedding water. "We shouldn't let mere words frighten us. In our present situation we would be irresponsible to let rhetoric outweigh the demands of reality."

"A lot of people have died over rhetoric in this waning century of ours, Doctor. Some of them willingly. What do you propose we do?"

"Come to terms with reality."

"You mean capitulate?" He couldn't keep the edge from

his voice. *I'm usually more reasonable than this. Maybe McKay's a bad influence on me.* He couldn't altogether repress a smile.

"I mean give some serious thought to resolving our differences with the Federated States. The world cannot survive any more superpower rivalry—and it does considerable violence to the language to term us a superpower in our present state.

"Even assuming the FSE does make demands on us, based on their as-yet hypothetical possession of this laser device, the responsible—the *caring*—response would be to use the opportunity to open a dialogue tuned to bringing us closer together. Instead of the macho reflex of sending out your overgrown Boy Scouts to try to foil the chairman. We've seen just where that kind of Wild West individualistic mythology leads us: disaster."

"It still sounds too much like surrender. I'm still a liberal, Dr. Connoly, but I am not a coward."

"Call off your dogs, Jeffrey."

Tiredly he shook his head."

Connoly rose, straightened her glasses on her snub of nose. "You are playing a dangerous game, Jeffrey. Someday it will catch up to you."

"It catches up to all of us, Doctor," he said, gazing out the window over the ruins of Washington, "sooner or later. In the meantime I do my duty and try to keep a pace or two ahead."

"Some security," Billy McKay said, staring up at the ceiling. It was invisible in the darkness. Might have been a thousand miles away. He had his fingers behind his tree-trunk neck.

Melissa Scowcroft raised herself on her elbows. Her blond hair hung in her face. Hair and darkness hid her eyes, which were green and slanted over Slavic-looking cheekbones. Shadow hid the way dainty, pale pink nipples crowned the pointed breasts swaying gently beneath her rib cage.

"Complaining?" She ran a finger over the slablike swelling of McKay's pectoral muscle. She was an aide to Marquerite Connoly, a model New Age bureaucrette, with a taste for wearing conservative skirt suits in the sort of colors they generally painted military matériel that accorded perfectly with late-twentieth-century American neo-Puritanism.

She also had a taste for garter belts and totally crazed rabbit sex that decidedly did not.

McKay grunted. "This is the goddam White House, after all. Yet here you come waltzing in here in the middle of the night as if it's the Motel 6. What's gonna keep some Syrian with a grudge and a great big cleaver from dropping by to talk to President Jeff?"

"I *am* staff, after all. I do have a certain degree of clearance."

She rose up onto her knees, shedding the blanket. "Still, if my presence offends your well-developed sense of security, I'll just be on my way. . . .

The light of the moon hanging like a big round piñata over the shacks of the Asian refugees and American vets in the Tidal Basin shone through the open window. It turned her body to silver and shadow. That was another thing about the New American Class: They did believe in keeping themselves in shape.

McKay growled again, with considerably more animation. "Come here, dammit."

The taut skin over her hips was as smooth and cool as polished steel. She held back, put fingertips to his chest.

"You be careful," she said.

"Always am," McKay grunted, starting to increase the pressure. You wouldn't think a paper pusher—one of Maggie's own, to boot—would have the same power international sex goddess Merith Tobias had exercised over him, to bring him snapping back in minutes like the randy linebacker for St. Joe's High he had been a decade and a half ago.

She shook her head. "This California thing, it could be a lot more dangerous than you think."

"Hey, danger is my business. I oughta get a card made with that for a motto. Come *here.*"

"No, seriously—oh, what the hell. Can I get on top?"

"What, again?"

CHAPTER FIVE —————————————————

"No, my dear," Yevgeny Maximov said, looking back over his shoulder. "Carry on talking." He turned his attention back to lining up his shot on the fourteen ball, looking for all the world like a bear in a burgundy dressing gown.

Nathalie Frechette made a mouth. To her it looked like a perfectly straightforward shot; the ball was all but on a line between the cue ball and the pocket, and all it took was just a kiss of back-English to avoid dropping the white. Hardly worth the production Maximov was making of it.

Oh, well; he was the boss. He did things his own way, as befit a strong man.

"Dr. Mallory reports that it will take some days to repair the malfunction that led to the beam detuning as it came on target, Excellency," she said.

Maximov made his shot. The cue ball curved ever so slightly, kissing the two ball before knocking the fourteen into the bumper. Maximov said something in Ukrainian that sounded impolite. But then, everything did in what the chairman of Federated Europe considered his native tongue.

"Oh! Your Excellency! I am so sorry."

He shrugged massively as he fished one of his own balls out of a pocket. "Think nothing of it, my dear. The scratch resulted from my own clumsiness, not your tidings."

He stepped back. "Please continue."

"Very well." She lined up her own shot briskly, fired, and produced a slight curve of her unpainted lips that was her closest customary approach to a smile as her ball sank. She was a woman in her late thirties, with a round face, snubbed nose, and hair of a startling burnt-umber color that her employer happened to know was quite natural. Everything about her appearance was natural, in fact; she wore no makeup. She dressed in a manner so severely plain as to be almost comical.

"The large-scale laser mounted in the satellite the Americans call Cygnus is, as I believe you are aware, of the free-electron variety, commonly designated FEL. FELs were once restricted to the longer, lower-energy wavelengths toward the infrared end of the spectrum. Advances in the late 1980s made possible a new generation of free-electron lasers, tunable through the entire visible spectrum and into the ultraviolet as well. This gave the advantage of being able to produce a beam of whatever wavelength was most suited to atmospheric conditions and the task at hand. Not incidentally, it also provided the Americans the fallback cover that the device was purely experimental in nature, intended for communications purposes, should its presence in the station be discovered."

She sank two balls as she spoke, then missed a shot. Maximov frowned pensively and rubbed his grizzled brown beard as he studied the table. The lighting in the recreation room here in the depths of his stronghold in *Schloss Ehrenbreitstein* was dim, by his command.

"You've certainly left me an assortment of targets, I'll grant," he rumbled. His voice was deep bass, his French impeccable.

She nodded absently. "In any event, the tuning mechanism really is experimental—very much so, in fact. Unless the Soviets were far more advanced than our intelligence indicates—"

"Unlikely."

"Precisely so. Which means the laser, which the Americans named Cygnus X-1, after the first supposed black hole to be discovered, is the most powerful broad-spectrum FEL yet devised. Inability to keep the proper wavelength at the high-energy end of the spectrum was apparently what kept the laser from being made operational by the outbreak of the Third World War. Oh, dear, you seem to have missed again."

"Astute as always, child." He stepped back. "So that's what our Dr. Mallory says. Is it possible the problem lies in his head . . . or his hands?"

She paled slightly, paused with her stick poised at an angle over the green baize board, like a flagpole jutting from a building.

He laughed indulgently, a sound like brick halves being shaken in an oil drum. "Have no fear, my dear. I will not hold you accountable for his actions. That's the problem with scientists. The ones who are truly accomplished in the esoteric fields are so rare that one must otherwise take them as one finds them. And, of course, our Colonel Hocevar and his men are on hand to ensure that our good doctor's agenda remains identical with ours, n'est-ce pas?"

"Y-yes, Your Excellency. Quite." Quickly she made her shot. It was the last solid ball except for the black one, which she promptly disposed of.

"I win," she announced with schoolgirl triumph, then quickly colored.

"So you do," Maximov said. He shook his heavy head. "I grow old, I fear."

"Oh, no," she said quickly. "Not at all."

He didn't show the smile he felt. The charming thing was, for all her efficiency and cold cunning, her occasional naïveté was as genuine as the color of her hair. She really thought he was immutable as the Pyramids.

"Not yet, perhaps. Not when I have the world left to conquer."

She laughed. He laughed too. She actually thought he was speaking hyperbolically of his great and noble design to unify the world and bring it the peace and harmony it had sought for millennia.

As a matter of fact, he could give a tenth-cc of sweat from his hairy balls for the great and noble principle of unifying the world. He just wanted to *rule* the damn thing. Idealism is a marvelous thing—as long as it isn't one's own.

As she returned her cue to the rack he said, "What of the ultimatum we planned to deliver to our American friends?"

"All depends upon how Your Excellency perceives President MacGregor. He possesses a weak type of personality. I believe he could be bluffed."

Maximov frowned and rubbed his beard. "I'm not so sure. He held up rather well when our President Lowell had him incarcerated in Heartland under sentence of death."

She made a deprecatory gesture. "That's mere endurance. Not that it is to be despised in its own right, but it might well have been symptomatic of the common American practice of wishful thinking, rather than indicative of moral courage. I think he would cave in if pressure were properly applied."

"Still, I prefer in this case to have the ability to back up any threats I may make. President MacGregor did, after all, take a hard line against the madman Morrigan's blackmail, although he did have us to help starch his spine."

"As you wish, Excellency. Now, if you will excuse me, my duties press me rather urgently."

He nodded dismissal. As she reached the door he said, "The longer we delay our ultimatum, the greater the chance of the Americans realizing that we have control of their orbital laser platform—if they haven't already, after our experiment in Spain."

"Our assets in place report Iskander's disappearance has caused great consternation in Washington, Mr. Chairman," Frechette said. "They have as yet delivered no details as to what the Americans know or surmise."

Maximov waved a hand. "Once they do apprehend the situation, the Guardians are certain to try to interfere, and we've ample reason to be wary of their resourcefulness."

He paused, smiled thoughtfully. "Of course, it is possible that those old friends of ours are in for a surprise. Those assets you referred to are very well placed to provide them one. But long experience has taught me never to count them out unless I actually see the bodies.

"Therefore, kindly convey a message to the good Dr. Mallory, my dear. He is to render the laser usable absolutely as soon as possible. I understand the exigencies of science, but I have my own. My patience is not inexhaustible."

He thought a moment, carefully chalking his own cue. "His daughter is well?"

"Yes, Excellency."

He nodded. "Perhaps it could be arranged that he speak to her then—*after* the laser is operational."

"Very well."

When she was gone, Maximov racked the balls again. He had never held with trying to make himself appear infallible and invincible; it was too much bother, and anyway, it didn't fool any but the most impressionable. And there were easier ways of impressing them. He belonged to the school of never letting others know what you really had—part of what Soviet military planners termed "cleverness," with what turned out to be undue optimism.

In the specific case of Nathalie Frechette . . . the girl had an overt case of hero worship for him. In itself that was no bad thing; it made it less likely that she would ever turn her position or her not inconsiderable intellect to the task of supplanting him, though he took no such thing for granted. Likewise, it helped her devote herself body and soul to the task of running his empire. She was the type who would do anything to please Daddy, and he was the most convenient one of those to hand.

Thinking again of the way her knee-length tweed skirt had tightened over her posterior as she bent to make her final shot, he entertained, not for the first time, the idea of having a go at her. She had that tight, full figure French women were noted for, and it took a considerable portion of her resources to keep herself looking dowdy and plain. And if he had simply walked up behind her, whipped her skirt up and her panties down, and plugged himself in, she would have done nothing at all except perhaps melt in ecstasy.

He banished the notion immediately, indulging himself in only the briefest of tactile and visual fantasies. He knew precisely how firm and blemish-free his aide's peach-round little rump was. The internal monitoring system within the converted castle overlooking the confluence of the Rhine and Moselle rivers was more comprehensive than even Frechette realized. It included pickups hidden in the women's locker room off the gymnasium, among other locations. Yevgeny Maximov had a touch of the voyeur in him, and the conviction that the best way to deal with his vices was to revel in them.

Only not this time. An American attorney he had retained once had mentioned to him that, as a fledgling fresh past the bar exam, he'd been taken aside by the senior partner of the firm that hired him and informed that it was strictly against policy to dip his pen in the company inkwell. Maximov still found that sound advice, not to mention amusing.

Working steadily but without hurrying, Maximov sank the striped balls, one after another. Then he ran the solids. Finally he pointed to a side pocket and dropped the eight ball into it with a three-carom shot.

There were some things even dear Nathalie didn't know about him. It was best that way.

CHAPTER
SIX ─────────────────────────────

"This is the way to travel," Billy McKay said approvingly, watching the Great Plains scroll by below, looking like a backdrop for a video game and showing about as much relief. You didn't see those funny green circles of irrigated land dotted all over everywhere, the way you used to before the war, but on the other hand, the terrain was showing a definite green tint with the onslaught of spring.

"If we'd been doing this on the ground, we'd be passing right through Reverend Forrie's backyard about now." The sprawl of Oklahoma City, Nathan Bedford Forrest Smith's capital, had passed off to their right not long ago. They hadn't wanted to cut it too close, just in case the current Prophet had turned up some high-altitude antiaircraft capability, but that was mainly just hedging their bets. Federal aircraft had overflown Okie City before without evoking any kind of hostile display.

Still, McKay was happy when the youthful ex-televangelist and current madman's stronghold was behind them. Melissa

Scowcroft's warning was still hovering around in the back of his brain. . . .

Naw. She's just a woman. They're always like that, getting worked up over nothing. Besides, Mike Levy was in the systems operator's chair above and behind him, nursing a board almost as powerful as the one in Mobile One, that would warn them if anything major was in the offing—say, a targeting radar locking on. Nothing like that was even fired up within a hundred-klick radius, though, unless Forrie had access to lots better gear than even his Effsee friends could have bestowed on him.

McKay sat back in the copilot's chair and felt that life was good. The sun hadn't rolled over the top of the sky yet, so that it was cool in the cockpit even though it was bright with that live-wire high-altitude morning light. Lieutenant Carey gave him a tentative smile from the seat next to him.

"Is it tough down there?"

"Naw. Not unless you mind a few thousand klicks of bad roads and permanent traffic jams, with road gypsies popping up every twenty minutes wanting your skin to make parachute pants out of, and the Faithful of the Church of the New Dispensation looking to kill you for Christ. You don't let that get to you, it's a lot like Disneyland, only dirtier, and they ain't got cute teenyboppers with big tits to stamp your tickets for you."

"Oh." It was obvious Carey didn't know quite what to make of Billy McKay. Oh, well—he wouldn't have to try for more than a couple more hours.

"What about you? What's it like to be a pilot for Armageddon Airlines?"

"Not bad. Takes some getting used to, but I guess the whole world's like that anymore."

Feeling mellow, McKay sat and let the lieutenant tell his story. He'd been a Herkie jock from the outset, attached to a Military Airlift Command wing out of Fort Bragg in North Carolina. He'd been on a troop shuttle run from the Midwest when the balloon went up for true. The Soviets had dropped a sub-launched missile on Bragg. In line with their dope dream of fighting a protracted war after a general thermonuclear exchange, they'd targeted the fort to damage America's conventional war-fighting capability. Well, it had, but the SS-N-6 would probably have done them more good if they'd dumped it on a missile silo somewhere.

"I was lucky," Carey explained. "Not only was I gone when the missile hit, but my wife Thelma and the kids were off visiting her people in Tennessee."

"You mean you still got a family?"

"Yes. Want to see?"

McKay said sure, though he didn't usually go in for snapshots that didn't have naked women in them. Thelma was an attractive, nondescript woman with glasses; the kids caramel-colored and smiling, the little girl with pigtails, the boy without.

"I'll be dipped," McKay said. The Guardians didn't run into many people with families these days. He wasn't sure why. The concept had an almost nostalgic ring to it, like all those shows about how great it had been to be a teenager in the fifties they'd had on during McKay's own seventies adolescence.

Carey returned the photos to his wallet and tucked it away, then continued his story. He'd put his ship down at a civilian airfield up the prevailing wind from Bragg—the sub-launched rocket hadn't been a ground burst, which as a general thing meant no fallout to speak of, but Carey and his passengers weren't eager to take chances. Then he'd gone to the base to try to help in the rescue operations and stand by in case the Soviets tried an invasion of the coast. The idea made McKay smile—and Carey, too, when he saw—but it hadn't been that funny at the time. American military men were taught to take Russian doctrine a lot more seriously than reality warranted, and the Soviets' war plans said they'd be following up their missiles with troops. One way or another, there was no way of knowing what the hell was really happening. Any possibility seemed real, as long as it was nightmarish.

The months after the war had been confused and dangerous—and what else was new? Carey managed to get in touch with his family within weeks, proving that his luck was still holding. They were spared the agony of uncertainty that tortured so many families in the U.S.—and Russia, and Europe, and more than a few other places worldwide.

When the Effsees came, the commander of the scratch transport wing he'd attached himself to declared for them. Not even McKay could bitch too much about that. A lot of the FSE expeditionary force were Americans, after all, and they did bring with them the last elected president of the United States, Wild Bill Lowell himself. Many good and patriotic Americans made the same decision.

Carey and his buddies had realized their mistake earlier than most, since they were set to work transporting plunder to seaport cities for transshipment onto FSE vessels. They deserted and fought in the underground on the East Coast, which was where he had met Nick Nicolaitis, his Lithuanian-born copilot.

Eventually the Effsees were driven out. By that time Jeff MacGregor was back in Washington, looking for more than a few good men. Carey had answered the call and been put to work helping recover transport planes like this one along the Eastern Seaboard.

"Now I've got my family living with me in Washington," he said. "The good Lord has really blessed us with good fortune."

He shook his head. "I can't help feeling I'm going to have to pay it back somehow."

"Don't worry about it," McKay said. "Just take what's offered and don't look back."

Carey showed him a shy smile. Then he frowned and craned his head forward, peering out the windscreen.

"Trouble up ahead, looks like," he said. "Smoke."

McKay squinted, saw a dirty white column climbing the sky to the northwest. It looked to be springing out of the general area where Oklahoma, Texas, Kansas, New Mexico, and Colorado all more or less came together around the Oklahoma panhandle.

"Yeah. Let's all count our blessings. Ours is, we ain't down there for the fire."

"What do you have, McKay?" asked Sam Sloan, materi-

alizing out of the rear of the plane, where he and Rogers had
been sacking out. "UFOs?"

"Unidentified nonflying assholes," McKay said, and
pointed out the smoke.

"Think a federal Texan or Texican flying column might be
beating up on some of Reverend Forrie's Mohawk boys?"
That was still the strangest bedfellow matchup the war had
made, turning the gangs of road gypsies, motorized nomads
for whom *The Road Warrior* was what *GQ* had been for yup-
pies, into allies of the Bible-pounding fundamentalist crazies
Forrie had inherited from First Prophet Josiah Coffin.

"Ha. Dream *on*. Some poor sodbusters eating death from
the Brothers of Mercy, more likely."

Sam shivered. The Guardians had had their own run-ins
with the Church of the New Dispensation's black-clad killer
elite. He changed the subject.

"Where's Casey gotten off to?" There was only so much
time even his heart could spend bleeding, after all, and it had
spent an awful lot of time doing so over the last two years.

McKay jerked his head back at the bulkhead behind.
"Sacked out in the crew bunk." You couldn't keep Casey far
from a cockpit, even when he needed to put some serious
rack time on the board.

Nick Nicolaitis turned up with a rack of steaming coffee
cups from the galley. He chased Sloan up out of the access
well into Turley's nav chair.

"This is what I've been reduced to with you big-time ce-
lebrity heroes on board," he complained. "I'm just a crummy
flight attendant. Me! A highly trained professional."

"Who ever heard of a flight attendant with a beard?" Mc-
Kay scoffed. "I don't call *that* professional. And look, you
didn't bring any goddam *sugar*, and now that I think about
it, you never offered us any *magazines*—I'm gonna write a
letter to the president of this crummy airline, is what I'm
gonna do."

"Write it to the CEO instead," Levy offered eagerly.
" 'Dear Dr. Connoly: Please fold this letter lengthwise and
stick it where the moon don't shine,' as Turley would say."

"Yeah. And we got no magazines, unless Turley has some of his crotch comics stashed under his board."

"Where's our token cracker, anyway?" Levy demanded. "Why isn't he at his board pretending he knows how to run it?"

"Logging Z's in the back," Nicolaitis said. "He says we ain't lost, and if we want to get that way, we don't need his expert help."

Carey showed very white teeth under his Air Force mustache in a nervous semi-smile. He was proud of his crew, but their carryings-on obviously were embarrassing him in front of their famous passengers. He was good troop, but too young and green yet to realize that that kind of non-reg bull-jiving was an indication of a tight team with high morale, not the opposite.

Nicolaitis handed McKay a Styrofoam cup with steam drifting out of it. "Got no cream, either, but I'm headed back to take a leak, so if you really want your coffee cooled off—"

"Get out of here!" Levy commanded. "These Balts are disgusting. Don't know why we let 'em in the country. They just move in, ruin a neighborhood with their lugubrious songs and smelly food, bring down property values. A scandal. Paul Ehrlich was right; we should have just slammed the Golden Door in their greasy faces."

Nicolaitis shot him an amiable finger and lumbered back to the head. "Was I being unfair?" Levy asked, looking around in mock distress. "I meant, except for their basketball players. Those Lithuanians play great basketball, and they do have natural rhythm. I mean, I can't be prejudiced, I'm Jewish."

McKay sipped his coffee. "Yaagh. I think the son of a bitch *already* pissed in mine."

"It must be old airline instant-coffee packets," Carey said apologetically. "That's all we could get in D.C."

"Our dear friend Dr. Connoly doesn't approve of coffee," Levy said. "She says it's an 'addictive substance.' Oh, well, what the hell? We can trade for some good Brazilian import in California."

"Doesn't anybody like Dr. Connoly?" Sam Sloan asked.

Carey glanced back over his shoulder at Levy. "No," the systems operator said. "Why? You sound as if your sense of fair play's been offended."

"Well," Sam said, "no."

Levy yawned, stretched, and slid out of his seat. "Yow. I have to stretch my legs a bit. Also, I think I'll roust out young Turley and make him work for a living for a while." He started back to the steps that led down from the flight deck.

There was a noise like ultimate thunder and the cockpit filled with smoke.

CHAPTER
SEVEN ─────────────────────

"Space turns us into odd creatures," the scientist said. "Into djinn from bottles."

Hovering behind his shoulder, his assistant smiled and gave a nervous little laugh.

"Whatever do you mean, Doctor?" she asked. Her English was flavored with a lilting Scandinavian accent. It would have been quite charming in its way, had he been susceptible to such things.

He gestured at the viewport before him. His features were mapped over a field of stars, as if his image were hanging out there in space like God's. This interstellar deity looked benignly ascetic, fit, and pink faced, and its hair had gone prematurely white. Winging side-whiskers made it look more like Monty Python's Eric Idle playing a gnome than anyone Charlton Heston might've portrayed.

But even in ghostly reflection there was something not quite right about that face. The features differed from the ones he had in calmer times been accustomed to shaving, mornings in his little flat in Geneva. The eyelids were puffy, the cheeks and long upper lip bloated, lending a touch of Fu Manchu Oriental menace to the face.

He turned to her, raised spatulate fingers to his cheek. "Thus . . ." He ran his hand down his body. "And thus. Our heads and upper bodies swell, our lower bodies and legs dwindle. Long enough up here and we'd simply trail away to wisps like cartoon genies, I shouldn't wonder."

Dr. Sylvie Braestrop looked at him, eyes wide and lips parted, not comprehending. The eyes were blue, the lips glossy. The hair that framed her face was the color of spring sunlight or some such rubbish. It was sometimes a trial to remember that she was an excellent technician and journeyman physicist. She was in some ways an idiot savant, he reckoned, utterly out of her depth in any waters but the great sea of science. What the Americans would call a nerd, in their usual sensitive way, though one seldom envisioned a *nerd* as looking as she did.

"You look wonderful to me, Doctor."

He thought about repressing a smile, did not. "I'd find myself grotesque," he said, "except I'm not all that enamored of the human form to begin with. We humans are wicked creatures; look at what we've done to our fair planet."

"But the viewport isn't facing the planet, Doctor."

He sighed. "Indeed." His own County Cork accent gave the word a musical sound.

He was lying, just a bit, for the sake of his own public image. He did find her form altogether pleasing, much as he hated to admit it. The figure in the blue coveralls with the Europe-map patch on the sleeve was full in the hips and strong in the legs, and inflated in the upper body without any help from zero-gee effects. Why she wasn't showing physiological effects from lack of gravity more, he couldn't say. Probably she did her exercises with the fanatical single-mindedness she brought to everything she did. He himself could barely be troubled to take the daily supplements to prevent loss of nerve fiber and the actual destruction of muscle tissue, the more permanent and insidious side effects of weightlessness.

Ah, but the devil Hocevar watches you like a hawk, doesn't he just? With his inevitable bland menace, the station's administrative head had made it explicit that Chairman Maximov regarded Dr. John Mallory as a priceless national asset, and would regard negligence of that asset's upkeep very sternly indeed.

Administrative head! Now that's a cute one, surely. Hocevar was there to make sure Dr. Mallory behaved himself. And alas, he had the means to see that he did just that.

He pushed away from the port—gently, gently, as he'd been trained years ago, before his tour in the Soviet *Mir* station. The name meant "peace," and hadn't *that* been empty?

The lab was partitioned from an American shuttle booster, a cylindrical section five meters wide and ten long, lined with padded panels of a sickly emergency-room green. In the middle of it a two-meter length of mechanism hung, clamped immovably by stays run to the hull. It looked like a collection of glass and chrome and plastic tubes of assorted lengths, arranged in parallel like a bundle of optical fibers. A coiled power bus had been made fast to one end, along with a Medusa's head of other clamps and cables.

The X-1 laser floated outside the station. It would only fit into the lab in its entirety if the partitions were removed. That was seldom necessary. Adjustments made to the device as a whole could generally be carried out by space-suited techs on a brief EVA. More detailed work could be performed inside without the need for suits; the laser was designed in modules that could be removed and brought through locks into the pressurized labs. As this one had.

He braked himself with a hand on one of the stanchions that secured the module, typed several sequences on a keyboard clamped to it. A humming filled the air, and a glow began to pulse rhythmically within the device. Mallory barely watched the results of the diagnostic program flicker past on the supertwist LCD screen. He knew what they'd be. He'd programmed in the "malfunction": he knew how to get rid of it.

For form's sake he waited until the diagnostic had run its course. "There we are, Sylvie. Tell Hocevar he may inform his chairman that his precious weapon will be back in service as soon as our technicians get the primary exciter reinstalled.'' He patted the white-plastic housing at the near end of the module.

She beamed. She thought the bug that caused the laser to power down just as it reached Iskander Bey's pavilion had been real. Fooling her had been a difficult task—she knew her lasers. But he knew his better. Which was fortunate; no matter how devoutly she worshiped him, how much she sympathized with his aims, she was so ingenuous, she simply would have burbled the truth in the commissary, where one of Hocevar's security detail was always hovering about like a persistent fly.

Security detail. That was another rich one. *What do we need securing from, floating away out here in space?*

''Dr. Hocevar will be so pleased,'' she exclaimed. ''And perhaps your Emily will be back from holiday tonight so that you can talk to her. Wouldn't that be a marvelous celebration?''

''Yes, child,'' he said slowly. ''Surely it would.''

You poor, naïve creature. She really believed the cover story, that his eleven-year-old daughter was on a camping trip in the Black Forest, and that was why she had been out of touch these last few days.

He wasn't quite sure why he'd arranged for the laser to lose its wavelength and power down just at the moment it would have eradicated Iskander Bey. An act of childish defiance; he wasn't even sure he had failed to kill Iskander. Certainly he was more in sympathy with Maximov's aims than that of a medieval Muslim fanatic.

Chairman Maximov wanted one world, after all. Where Dr. John Mallory parted company with him was at Maximov's insistence that he himself should administer the united globe.

It was touch and go whether the Earth could heal herself after man's most recent folly—or whether indeed the war had been a drastic blessing, putting an end to the ever-increasing cycle of despoilment and pollution. Whatever the truth, the lesson had been driven home that governing Earth was too vital and complex a task to be handled by anything but a committee of the world's top scientists.

Mallory had hoped Maximov would be able to use the threat of the captive American laser to bring the world to heel without it becoming necessary to actually put the weapon *in the chairman's hands*. The optimal scenario was for Maximov to obtain power with minimal loss of life—Mallory was a compassionate man—and then give way to a proper scientific regime. Both halves of the equation would be enormously complicated by Maximov's having immediate access to the laser.

But if he was unsure why he had disabled the laser at just that moment, he was not uncertain at all as to why he had repaired it as rapidly as he could without arousing suspicion.

Emily, he thought, *my sole love, my soul's love. I hope at least it's a decent sort of prison they're keeping you in.*

And have patience, dear child. For one of these fine days the good chairman and his damn mastiff Hocevar will overlook one slight detail. They're not scientists; they've not the mental discipline not to make a mistake, soon or late.

And on that day we shall be free. You, the planet that gave you birth, and maybe, if Fortune smiles, even your poor father.

CHAPTER
EIGHT ─────────────────────

A plane is a lot like a man: it takes a lot to kill one.

McKay knew at once there'd been an explosion, and a big one, as much by feel as anything else. He registered at once that there was no radical change to the Hercules' flight. That was good—it meant that the whole tail section wasn't gone, say, which would have sent the beast into an unrecoverable flat spin *right now.* .

It was about the only good news. The board in front of the copilot's chair was an uninterrupted blaze of red. Billy McKay was under no illusions that the apparently normal flight was going to continue for any length of time.

Carey seemed to be settled down in his seat, studying his red-lit panel. *Good. Cool head.* Behind him, McKay heard a commotion from Sloan and Casey. The former fighter jock's burned-in reflex automatically sent him for the controls when he felt a plane in trouble. Like all the Guardians, when the shit hit the fan he came instantly awake, but he seemed to have his foot in Sloan's ear as he tried to clamber out of the cramped crew bunk.

It was good fortune that three of them were up here when the explosion happened in back. But that left—

"Tommy," McKay yelled, "report! Are you okay?"

"I'm fine, Billy," Tom said over the Guardians' communicator net. Transmitted through the small bone-conduction speaker taped to the bone behind McKay's ear, Tom's voice sounded as if it were talking in the back of his head. The ex-Green Beret sounded as calm as if he were discussing which pair of tennis shoes to buy. *"Just a bit shaken up."*

"What happened?"

"Big explosion in the central section of the airplane. There's a lot of smoke back here, and the area around the wing roots seems to be burning pretty fiercely. It's getting hot."

Over his shoulder, McKay heard Levy shouting into his own intercom headset. He didn't seem to be having any success.

"What about the flight crew?"

"Turley's fine. He was back here with me near the ramp. But Nick was just heading back from the john when the blast hit."

That didn't sound too good. The world outside the Plexiglas tipped as the big plane started to fall off on one wing. That didn't *look* too good, and McKay turned to Carey to see what he proposed to do about it.

The pilot was slumped down in his chair with his head hanging to one side and a faraway look in his eyes.

"Shit," McKay said. By reflex, he grabbed Carey's shoulder. The pilot tipped forward onto his steering yoke.

There was a jagged hole in the back of his uniform, spang between the shoulder blades. The stain spreading out from the hole looked black on the blue cloth. There was a corresponding hole in the back of his seat.

"Oh, Jesus!" Levy exclaimed. "Lynn! *Lynn!*"

"Get a hold of yourself," McKay said gruffly. Levy seemed steady enough in normal circumstances, but under these, McKay was taking zero chance of letting panic take hold.

First things first. He grabbed his own yoke and reached over to flip the switch to enable the copilot controls. Feeling

his scrotum trying to crawl up inside his asshole, he brought
the plane back to level flight. As a result of the comprehen-
siveness of his Guardians training he could fly the Hercules,
though not real well. Especially not well enough to keep it
under control when it was badly hurt and the damage was
almost certainly growing worse with every accelerated beat
of his heart. Even he could feel the big ship was in trouble,
from the way it responded beneath his hands. It seemed to
be shuddering in terminal agony.

"Casey, get your foot out of Sam's ear and take over here."
If anybody could keep the wounded Herkie from doing a last
long Brody into the Llano Estacado, it was Case. "Levy,
what the fuck happened? Missile?"

"Negative. The *Pig's* got three-sixty radar coverage. We're
all alone up here." After his initial shock at seeing his commander dead, he was the total professional again.

"Could it have been a malfunction?" Sam asked, surren-
dering his chair to let Casey climb into the seat McKay had
vacated.

"Not something this big," Casey said, settling into the
chair. It took him a moment; he had already shrugged into a
parachute harness. "We have a major problem."

Casey naturally belonged to the Chuck Yeager laconic
school as a news commentator. If he thought their troubles
were "major" that was enough for McKay. They were officially in *deep shit*.

He headed aft, pausing only to snag the fire extinguisher
mounted on the bulkhead above down the access well, and
then went down the steps to the door to the cargo bay.

When he was a bald kid on leave after completing boot
camp, he'd tried playing Dungeons & Dragons for the first
and only time. The Dungeon Master was the only one in the
group he really knew, a creepy kid named Schwartz who
subsequently became a minor drug kingpin—more like a
dukepin, maybe. McKay and four of these fools he'd barely
met had their characters snooping and pooping through this
big old castle. They'd come to a door and detected something
on the other side. The other kids told McKay to go first because he was the Warrior. And he did, because not only was

he the Warrior, he was a sunburned kid with all the hair
shaved off his head who'd spent the last six weeks running
up and down hills screaming "Kill! Kill!" and had to prove
he was badder than anybody. Also, he'd been drinking steadily for eight hours.

So anyway, he opens the door to charge through, and this
thing called a Hellhound, which had craftily been waiting on
the other side in hopes of idiots like him, goes *fazoom*! And
there is nothing left of Billy McKay the Ultimate Warrior
except a pair of boots with smoke sort of trailing out the tops
of them.

And the kid playing the Magic User strokes the wispy beard
which is competing for face space with his zits and says,
"Gee, I'm glad it was *Billy*."

So naturally McKay had to pound him, and after that nobody asked him to play D&D anymore. Just when he was
thinking he could get to like it.

This was a lot like the game. He whipped open the door,
and fortunately his reflexes were good, because a big belch
of flame went *fazoom*! just like that fucking Hellhound, and
he was quick enough jumping back to save most of his eyebrows.

The air was mostly rushing from the nose of the airplane
into the fire, so he was able to duck through then, squirting
CO_2 liberally around. The middle of the aircraft looked like
Hell on furlough. It was just a solid mass of yellow fire back
there. If McKay had been toying with any doubts that they'd
been sabotaged, that settled them then and there. He may not
have been a pilot but he'd spent a whole lot of his life in
C-130s. He knew damn well there was no fuel tanks inside
the fuselage or even next to it; fuel was stored in tanks in the
wing outboard of the engines, and in auxy tanks beneath the
wings.

Incendiary, he thought. He would have accomplished as
much against that inferno by whipping out his dick and whiz-
zing on it, but he sprayed a lot more foam around anyway.
Of course, it did no good.

"Tom, what's your status?" he asked.

"Turley and me got fire extinguishers, but they ain't doing much."

"Same here." He thought quickly, then asked the question he wasn't sure he wanted the answer to.

"You got parachutes back there?"

"All over the airplane. These boys believe in being prepared."

"Thank God for small fucking favors. This airplane is never gonna last."

"I was going to mention that. Out the ports we can see flames coming off the starboard wing."

"Fuck *us*." That really tore it. It had been multiple charges, more than likely. Detonated by a timer—or from a signal broadcast from the surface? They *were* over Forrie Smith territory. . . .

No time for that shit now. His face felt sunburned. "Blow this flying pop stand, Tom, as in now. We'll be right along as soon as we see what we can salvage."

He threw the extinguisher into the flames. While the goddess of discord had been handing out minor concessions, She had arranged that they actually came in the front door this morning, right into the well aft of the flight deck. Guardians though they were, they were still human; they secured their gear just on the other side of the bulkhead, right at the front of the cargo bay. McKay grabbed a couple of rucksacks and hustled back to the cockpit.

Levy and Sam had been checking over the flight deck. A half dozen fragments propelled by the blast had punched through the bulkheads, but only the one Carey copped hit anybody. McKay tossed the rucks down.

"Give a hand, Sam. We're getting off this bus."

"Billy, Turley says he's not going without Carey giving the word to abandon."

McKay muttered a couple of choice words about people who picked the wrong moment to come all-over hard-core. "Tell him he's got a long wait. Carey's dead."

"I'm in command of the ship now," Levy said, obviously picking up enough from McKay's contribution to get the drift. "Tell him to get the hell out. You boys better 'chute up, too;

I don't think even Lieutenant Wilson can hold her much longer.''

McKay was passing Levy's order along to Turley. "Casey can fly anything."

"Not for long, Billy," Casey said. "We're losing aileron control. And if the wing tanks go, we're going to, like, do a great imitation of a meteorite."

Sam came back with one of the secondary packs they'd been toting along as Tom Rogers reported that he and the navigator were going out the rear emergency escape hatch. "This is everything we're going to get. Fire's too bad."

Usually in a case like this McKay would make some crack about what a wimp black-shoe Navy boys were. Instead he tossed Sloan a parachute.

"Fuck it. This beast's a bomb."

The plane was starting to buck and weave. The cockpit was full of fumes that seared eyes and throat. It was getting very warm.

Sloan hefted a ruck. "Will she fly straight enough for us to ditch? She's rolling like an LST in a Cape Hatteras storm."

"No way," Levy said. "She can take a lot, but she's taken all she can. I'll hold her."

"No," said Casey Wilson. "I've got her."

So everybody stood around for a precious couple of heart-beats, staring at him, because it was obvious that the plane was coming out of the air in seconds—whether in one piece or many, no one knew.

"Forget it, Case," McKay said. "We need you. Guardians ain't expendable." The implication was that Levy *was*, but the systems engineer was standing there nodding his head like an eager dog, all filled with self-sacrifice.

Casey waved his hand. "*Go on,* dammit. Take my rifle. Leave my pack in Carey's lap."

That was a weird set of directives if McKay had ever heard one, but there was no more time for bullshit. Besides, he was shocked; Casey never cussed.

"Right," McKay said.

Levy's disappointment at missing martyrdom didn't seem too long-lived; he took off for the crew entry door in a hell of a hurry. There was an emergency hatch above the access well, but McKay suspected it was for getting out in case of a water landing. You went out that way now, the only two ways to go were straight back into the fire and down into the draft of those hungry black propeller blades. As it was, McKay wasn't just nuts about the prospects of missing the props from the door. Those props reminded him an awful lot of those meat-slicing machines they used to have at Arby's.

Sloan passed Casey's ruck forward from the crew bunk, where Casey had dragged it in an unusual fit of anal retentiveness—being around airplanes did that to him. McKay dumped the pack on Carey and tried to figure out how to make the lengthy sniper's rifle fast to his parachute harness.

Fuck it, I'll do it on the run. "Case," he said, and his throat was dry.

Casey waved a hand. With his inevitable yellow Zeiss shooting glasses and his tour cap, he looked as if he were just taking the old Piper Cub out for a Sunday spin above the Sierra Nevada. "I'll be fine." As if to give him the lie, another explosion cracked inside the cargo compartment.

McKay nodded and ran for the hatch. Levy had ditched already. Sam Sloan gave McKay a stark look from the whistling doorway. McKay waved him on. He vanished.

The bulkhead between the well and the cargo bay was glowing almost white. The heat played over the side of McKay's face like a spray of acid.

He paused to make sure Casey's rifle was going to clear the door. Then he braced and threw himself out of the plane with all his strength, hoping like hell to clear the props.

He tucked himself into a ball as the wind hit him. He heard the drone of the engine whistle to a crescendo, felt the awful tug of suction from the whirling, curved black blades. And then he was clear, tumbling over and over.

Above him he heard another explosion.

CHAPTER
NINE

The wind was cold and cut through McKay's camouflaged jumpsuit like an oxyacetylene torch. Once he got his innards convinced he was out of reach of those evil propellers, he extended his arms and legs to slow his tumble and tried to get his glide under control.

In a moment he was sailing right along like Rocky the Flying Squirrel. The Hercules had been cruising along above thirty thousand feet to take advantage of the optimum lift-to-air resistance ratio, so he shouldn't be meeting up with the planet any time too soon.

He looked up. The Hercules seemed cocooned in flame along its entire length. He looked for a parachute above him, or a dark, hurtling speck—some sign that Casey Wilson, his friend and comrade, had made it out of the blazing aircraft.

Because if he ain't made it out now, he thought grimly, *he ain't never gonna make it.*

McKay let himself glide for a time, willing himself not to feel the cold. He tried to scan the landscape below, without the greatest success. A jump like this really required goggles. The wind was painfully drying his eyes.

He managed to see enough to realize that picking a landing spot wasn't going to be much of an issue. The land below rolled so gently as to appear to be totally flat from above. From having been on the ground in the Texas Panhandle before, he guessed it would probably look pretty flat from ground level, too, though that was an illusion. There was a lot more dead ground in the Plains than you might think.

The black ribbon of a surfaced road ran well off to his right, too far to be a consideration. He could make out what seemed to be a couple of farms—small, lonely clumps of buildings, one or maybe two flanked by the only trees in sight. Finding a spot to put down wasn't going to be much of a challenge: no woods, no big stretches of standing water, none of the worst landing hazards parachutists faced. The biggest danger was finding a high-tension line that hadn't been put underground before the war. *That* could ruin his day, but in between blinking tears across his eyes he couldn't spot any of the distinctive silver-white towers.

Wind and momentum seemed to be carrying him toward a short line of tall, thin trees of the kind that generally served Plains homesteads as windbreaks. Beyond stood a few small frame structures and a mound that suggested the aboveground part of an earth-sheltered house. He decided to go with the flow and make for that.

He judged that they had flown clear of both federal Texan and Oklahoman airspace before ditching. While Forrie's boys raided west with some frequency, neither Washington nor Dr. Morgenstern in California had picked up any intelligence to indicate Okie City had seized any of New Mexico. That meant it was probably safe to land openly and get in touch with the locals, see about promoting food, water, shelter, care for any injuries the survivors of the bombing might have picked up, maybe even transport—if their luck was truly in. It wouldn't be, but he was entitled to hope.

Below him, first one parachute bloomed into a colorful rectangle, then another. Sam Sloan and Levy both still seemed to be functional, at least.

As he fell between them he was gratified to see a look of startled concern plainly visible on Sloan's face. *Good to know the Navy boy cares,* he thought.

About then it occurred to him that their communicators were probably still in working order. "McKay," he said, the wind whipping the words away from his mouth but the tiny microphone taped to his larynx transmitting them clearly to any Guardians in range. "Report if you can."

He pulled the rip cord and rode out the shock as the chute deployed. He ran a quick visual check to make sure the parafoil was properly open—not that there was anything he could do about it if it *wasn't*, since he didn't have a backup, but that was the way he'd been trained, and anyway, the subject held a certain morbid fascination for him.

"Sloan here," came back in his ear as he confirmed that the chute seemed to be just fine.

"Roger, Sloan. Anybody else?"

Pause. Nothing. *"I think Tommy's out of range. Casey— uh, maybe he's too busy to talk."*

"I'm making for the stand of trees there a klick or two west-southwest," McKay said. "Follow my lead, and try to keep Levy tagging along."

Another pause. "I see them, McKay, and will comply."

Moments later Billy McKay saw the Super Hercules streak down the sky like a meteorite, several kilometers off to his right. He winced at the terminal explosion. *Poor Casey.*

He'd slung the former fighter jock's long Remington sniper's rifle in a real ad hoc way across the front of his body. It wasn't all that much lighter or more wieldy than his Maremont M-60E3 machine gun, which, at a guess, was currently melting into slag along with the rest of the 130 somewhere in northeastern New Mexico.

What a crock, he thought. *Casey buys it, and I wind up humping his goddam* rifle *all the way across the Wild fucking West.*

He was getting mighty near the planet. The fields below looked as if they had been plowed or turned over or whatever some time before, but if anything had been planted in them

it wasn't showing for the weeds. He worked the lines to avoid
a skeletal windmill that was clattering and squealing on un-
lubricated bearings, and came in a hundred meters short of
the trees in the sort of running landing he'd have chewed the
ass off a boot for trying in jump training. It risked a real old-
fashioned ankle busting, but he didn't want to try to roll over
that damn rifle.

He spilled the air from the foil before the wind could pull
him off his feet again, and was shedding the harness as Sam
and Levy made textbook hit-and-roll touchdowns within
twenty meters.

"Show-offs," he said. He started walking toward the others. They both appeared unhurt, but suddenly Sloan started
dancing around, as if he'd dropped onto a fire-ant nest.

What the fuck's with *you*?'' McKay asked. ''You bang your
head on the way out?''

Sloan pointed up in the cloudless sky. ''Billy, *look*!''

Casey Wilson loved airplanes more than anything. When
he was just a surfer boy, the tanned and privileged son of
Southern California techie parents, he'd stop whatever he was
doing and watch any time an airplane, any airplane, flew by.
Sometimes he got bonked on the head by the volleyball, which
would make all the huskier jock types hoot at him. They
didn't hoot quite so much when all the bikini bunnies crowded
around to cuddle him and ask him if he was all right.

Casey loved airplanes so much, he was able to get accepted
for fighter-pilot training, even though he didn't fit the
standard-issue loud, arrogant, drinking-and-driving super-
jock template. In a rare fit of perception the powers-that-be
recognized that he had every foot-pound of the competitive
fury that drove his more extroverted classmates. In the air he
was more aggressive than anybody, more aggressive than
anybody most of his instructors had ever *seen*. He flunked
out of live dogfight training, Aggressor school, on his first
go-round because of his insane bravado. But his technical
proficiency was so extreme that he got a rare second chance.
Having learned to tone himself down with the disciplines of
t'ai chi he passed at Mach 2.

The world being the way it is, the little boy who so loved airplanes turned out to be the most proficient destroyer of them in modern times. A fighter pilot in the Werner Voss mode, he was an excellent tactician, consummate edge-of-the-envelope flier, lethally precise marksman. In three weeks in the Middle East he had shot down seven enemy aircraft—five of them in one twisting, blazing, gut-clenching sortie. After that the American high command jerked him from combat, terrified of the propaganda value should some Syrian missile crew get lucky and put a SAM into him—or, say, an entire wing of Soviet "adviser" pilots try to set him up for a gang fuck. That was one of the reasons the Israelis were so cagey about letting out the names of their own top guns.

Casey was desperate to get back into the combat of the sky. It was the purest form known of communion with aircraft, the purest flying. The only thing that came near was flight testing. He was trying to lobby his way into that when one-eyed Major Crenna found him.

Being a Guardian wasn't flying—mostly, anyway. But it did offer challenges of its own.

As his buddies were diving for the exits Casey Wilson was fiddling around one-handed in his pack—he could control the plane with one hand, to the extent he could control it at all. The Hercules was incredibly tough and inherently stable, not a high-strung, neurotic fighter where you punched out at the first flash of red on the board. But she was dying. He could feel it in his soul, and the knowledge tore at him.

Just as he reckoned his buddies were clearing the plane, he felt the next explosion tear the guts out of the airplane. *Starboard wing tank,* he thought. Miraculously the Herkie was still under control, but it had only seconds of life left.

The fingers of his left hand found what they were searching for: a hard shape like a stick or baton maybe half a meter in length. As Billy McKay had been a few moments ago—or a few eternities, depending on one's perspective—Casey was grateful for the Guardians' exhaustive cross training. His fingers made the necessary adjustments to the disk fixed at the midpoint of the stick by touch, relying on calibrated clicks to tell him what he'd done. When he had it ready, he snapped it open into an *X* shape with a flick of the wrist, peeled plastic strips off the arms with his teeth, and slapped the exposed adhesive against the windshield in front of Carey's corpse. Then he hauled his ruck over on to his own lap and leaned *way* over to the right with his left arm protectively raised beside his face and was very glad he was wearing the shooting glasses.

The X-frame explosive was an old antiterrorist standby. It was designed to take out doors and windows with a small, contained blast that did not endanger people even right beside it. Since it was meant to be used in seconds-count situations, when the boys in the balaclavas were ready to bust in and start shooting Iranians before they woke up and began offing hostages, you could set the attached timed detonator to as little as five seconds, which Casey had done.

It was the longest five seconds he'd ever lived through. The flames were actually licking into the cockpit now, the seat back was hot behind him, and Carey's chair was smoking. Worse, he could *feel* the longerons and fuselage frames, heated white by the ferocious flames, beginning to melt and give way.

The explosive cracked off. It wasn't a very loud sound, especially over the moan of the engines and the fire's roar, but it was piercing, with lots of supersonic crack in it. The panel of Plexiglas in front of Carey neatly blew out.

Working as deliberately as if he were preflighting his personal gear safe and sound in the hangar, Casey made his ruck fast to the chute harness with a bungee cord. The wind boiled in on him, cold and furious. In the face of its force he felt total calm, controlling his breath as his Chinese martial discipline taught. Control your breathing, his teachers said, and you likewise control your mind and body. He had found this to be true.

He pulled back on the controls. The doomed Hercules had been descending steadily. Now Casey wanted the nose up to kill speed.

He felt the aileron control go beneath his hands. But the plane had pulled into a brief climb. It should be enough. . . .

Casey pushed his ruck out the hole his X-charge had made in the windshield. Then he followed, clambering unapologetically over the unfeeling Carey.

As he intended, the wind had been slowed by his speed-killing maneuver. It tore at him with angry, cold fingers, but he held on, following the rucksack over the black mound of the radome and off into space.

It took him little time to control his tumble. Once he did, he looked up. It took an effort of will to do so: if he'd misjudged and pulled the nose up too steeply, the odds were good he'd see the Hercules hurtling right down on him, forty tons of flaming doom.

He had judged perfectly. He saw the Herkie falling back to level flight, tipping away as a fresh series of explosions sheathed it completely in flame. It went into a long dive to the northwest, steepening as it went. The right wing folded just before impact in a broad field. The plane blew up with a fireball that was dazzling even in the bright spring sunlight.

He sighed, shook his head sadly. In a lot of ways he felt like a doctor who'd lost a patient. It happened—he'd had planes go down beneath him before—but you were never happy about it. Even when you never had a chance of keeping your subject alive.

He looked down. The Hercules had lost almost ten thousand feet from the instant of explosion. Below, he saw the bright rectangles of his comrades' chutes. Three of them. He nodded in satisfaction. Billy, Sam, and the systems engineer had all gotten away clean.

To deploy the chute this high up—just passing twenty thousand feet—would expose him to a lot of cold. Better to ride it out until he was much closer to the ground. As a Guardian, he was expert in HALO techniques—high-altitude, low-opening parachuting—but there was no need for anything that extreme.

He let himself relax and enjoy the sensation of falling free.

When Casey touched down, McKay was standing among the windbreak poplars smoking a cigar and holding the Remington 700X rifle by the sling. He acknowledged the youthful-looking Guardian's arrival with a grunt and a nod.

"Good to see you could join us," he said. "Otherwise it don't look like one of those days when it pays to get out of bed."

He gestured with the cigar. It was a recent prewar semi-subterranean farmhouse, all right. But what had looked to McKay, up in the air with the wind in his eyes, like a potential source of help was in fact a burned-out shell. The sheds and chicken coop looked pretty trashed-out, too, from closer range.

"I think we may have, like, a couple more problems, Billy," Casey said as he finished collapsing his chute and folding it under his arm.

"That wasn't what I needed to hear."

"McKay!" Sloan called. "We have company on the way."

McKay looked east, where Sloan was pointing. A line of vehicles had appeared on the horizon, which, owing to a slight swell in the fallow farmland, was nearer than it appeared. At least one truck and half a dozen motorcycles.

McKay could make out the outlandish outfits of the riders, and the fact that they were heavily armed. As he stood and stared they rolled forward, the wind carrying their triumphant cries before them like banners.

CHAPTER
TEN

"Can I have my rifle, Billy?" Casey Wilson asked.

"My goddam pleasure." McKay tossed him the big Remington. Casey caught it as casually as if McKay had been flipping his tour cap to him. The fancy computerized sight was pretty invulnerable, and even the more conventional shoot-through glass optics were well shockproofed. "Time to hit the trees. You and the Navy boy get ready to fire up the bad guys. Levy and I will sit on our thumbs until they're close enough to see the reds of their eyes."

Before Casey's arrival, his two buddies and the orphaned flight crewman had begun a quick inventory of their assets. The good news was that Sloan's Galil Short Assault Rifle with the M-203 40-mm grenade launcher slung under the barrel and the attendant multipocket vest-o'-grenades had reached ground safely.

The bad news was everything else.

They had among them three claymores and a dozen grenades, white phosphorus, stun and CS gas, a few blocks of C-4 with assorted timers and command detonators, and some gadgets like the door- and window-buster Casey had used to blow out the Herkie. It wasn't easy to see how those last were going to come in real handy, unless some of the road gypsies freaked out and decided to hole up in a shed or something.

McKay's M-60, of course, had gone the way of *Tyrannosaurus rex*, in company with the Super Hercules. One of the counterterrorist special MP5 machine pistols, the kind with the silencer built right in that they carried for close-in and quiet work, had survived, which was something. On the other hand, in spite of standing orders for aircrew operating out of Washington, Mike Levy was not wearing a side arm.

"I can't believe you aren't wearing a fucking *piece*," McKay said as they ran for the trees. "Didn't you ever see any after-the-Holocaust movies?"

"Only *The Day After*," Levy replied. He was carrying Casey's collapsed chute to stash with the others in the burned-out house, so it wouldn't attract any more attention than it already had. "It filled me with so much despair, I figured it was futile to carry a gun."

"Fuck," McKay said. "Borrow Sloan's side arm. If you get into trouble, you can use it as a signal mirror."

With a pained expression Sloan pulled his much-maligned Colt Python .357 Magnum from his shoulder holster. Its nickel-plate finish glinted in the hot New Mexican sunlight as he handed it off to Levy.

Casey paused to drop his ruck and pull out his Kevlar vest. His two comrades already had theirs unpacked and on; Levy was going to have to work extra hard not to get hit. He shrugged into the bulletproof vest and looked for a place to go to ground.

The line of trees ran from north to south for about thirty meters. They were the best available cover; if the defenders positioned themselves among the buildings, the trees would screen them from their targets. McKay bit dirt on the northern end, Sloan the southern. Casey took up position to McKay's right. When Levy returned, he went to ground between Casey and Sloan. That gave flank protection to Casey, who as sniper had to concentrate on long-range work—and in any event wasn't very accurate inside fifty meters—and the unknown quantity Levy.

The wind blowing in their faces was hot and dry. After almost freezing his balls off on the way down, McKay was glad for the shade of the poplars. This was clearly not good country for trees, since there weren't many others to speak of, but these seemed to be doing just fine. Maybe the heavier precipitation since the One-Day War agreed with them. He could always ask Dr. Mahalaby out at New Eden in California, if he ever happened to give that much of a fuck.

He had the extra ripstop bag they'd rescued, with six spare box magazines and four boxes of ammo for the MP5. Five hundred ten rounds, counting the thirty in the piece's mag. Since this was a limited-issue .45-caliber model—.45 rounds started out subsonic, which meant you could silence them fairly effectively without sacrificing shocking power or changing the aim point, the way downloaded 9-mm did—he could use rounds from his spare pistol magazines too. Call it almost six hundred, all found.

Sounded like a lot, but a good firefight could eat every cartridge inside six minutes.

McKay had been rated an expert marksman from his boot-camp days, and had gotten cured of hosing off whole magazines in inaccurate full-auto panic fire by about his second dose of combat in the southern Mediterranean hot zone. He knew how to stretch his ammo as far as it could possibly go. But sooner or later the Heckler & Koch machine pistol's bolt would click home on an empty chamber, and that would be damn well that.

And the road gypsies kept on coming. There were a good twenty of them streaming toward them now in a wide, ragged skirmish line. McKay's palm itched with need for his Maremont. Couldn't he just winnow those fuckers with that thing?

As it was, Casey had the only weapon that would reliably reach them at this range, seven hundred meters and closing. Even with the improved 5.56 rounds, you couldn't expect Sloan's SAR to touch them up much past five, and 5.56 did jack against vehicles at any range you cared to name. If the road gypsies played it conservative and smart, surrounded them and tried sniping them deliberately, they could be in a world of hurt even if Casey never fluffed a shot.

Fortunately *conservative* wasn't exactly road gypsy style. Neither was *smart*.

Nobody's binoculars had arrived intact. That meant relying on Casey to spot what exactly the bad guys had with his Star Wars scope.

"One vehicle, Billy," he reported. "Carryall. Kind of."

"I can *see* that, Case. Give me news."

"Looks like a couple MG mounts on the carryall. M-60, I think. Otherwise small arms . . . no, wait, got a sidecar with, like, another machine gun mounted. M-249, I bet."

McKay would bet too. The 7.62-mm M-60 had kind of a potent recoil to fire off a motorcycle sidecar. The M-249 fired the smaller, 5.56 NATO round and could cause them plenty of grief if the gypsies parked to fire it. More likely they were going to want to play *Rat Patrol* and blaze away at full throttle, which meant it would basically take the personal help of Forrie Smith's God for them to score any hits. If the carryall mounted two M-60s, though, it could be very painful, even if the gypsies fired on the move.

Obviously Casey was thinking along the same lines. "Shall I take the carryall's driver? Or gunners?"

Time was getting short. The road gypsies were rolling slow right now, obviously enjoying stretching this thing out, but the range was closing.

"Negative," McKay said. "Don't scare 'em. Let 'em come in range of Sloan's thump gun, if they will. Hit the sidecar bike, anytime you're ready. Sam, be ready to nail that truck the instant it's close enough."

Sloan's reply came over the headphone. Casey's came in the heavy *thump* of a sound-suppressed 7.62 round going off. The sidecar bike's driver tossed up two gauntleted hands and rolled off the seat. The gunner grabbed frantically for the bars as the bike veered.

At first that was the only response. While you just could not drain all the sound out of a 7.62 round—the supersonic bullet cracked like a mother when it passed anything, for one thing—a suppressor could make it hard to tell where a shot was coming from. Or even that one had been fired, several hundred meters upwind with a score of engines growling all around. The riders to either side of the sidecar machine seemed mainly concerned about veering away and not running into it.

But one big puke, in some kind of shiny space suit thing with long tassels streaming from the shoulders, who rode near the heavily modified carryall in the center of the line was more alert. He waved his hand and apparently yelled something.

A fence crossed their path, three strands of barbed wire. The carryall parted it with a twang that carried all the way to the defenders. The engine rumble shot up in volume as the gypsy riders cranked their throttles all-out and streamed forward through the gap. Fire stabbed from the muzzles of the carryall guns.

Splinters rained down on McKay's head and shoulders as a burst ripped the trees a meter above him.

"They have M-60s, Billy," Casey's voice came over the communicator.

"No shit?" The vehicle was falling behind the bikes as they sprinted forward in a roil of dust. His heart tried to crowd into his throat at the thought that it might intend to stop and fire them up from outside the four-hundred-meter range of Sloan's grenade launcher.

But no, it just didn't have the pickup the bikes did. One of the guns fired again, and a line of tan dust geysers spurted into the air forty meters short of the windbreak. Casey's rifle thumped again. The sidecar gunner, who had just gotten a grasp on the outrageously upswept handlebars and brought the machine more or less under control, let go and slumped back in the car.

"Hit the son of a bitch with the shiny long johns next, Case," McKay directed via communicator. No sooner had he heard the thump of Casey's rifle than the target vanished in a fold of ground. It wasn't in Casey's nature to cuss, so McKay did some for him.

Another M-60 burst splashed dirt in his face. *Those fucks are getting too close for comfort.*

Fortunately one of the carryall-mounted guns was busy working over the buildings beyond the trees. Casey's suppressor took care of flash, too, not that it was all that visible in the daylight. The bad guys weren't going to get any help spotting their targets. That was a disadvantage to the Maremont, you had to admit—you touched that puppy off, at night it made a fireball the size of a Subaru, and kicked up a giant cloud of dust and debris in the daytime, letting entirely everybody know where you were.

McKay would've taken one anyway, somehow.

Like all road gypsy transport—all road gypsies, for that matter—the carryall's appearance had been extensively modified. It had been covered with slanting armor plates, with just a slit for the driver to look through. Whatever precisely it had started as, it was a double-decker now, with one gunner beside the driver and the other up on a sort of armored box. The weird-looking vehicle sported black banners with skulls on them and what looked like whip antennas, though they might have been for show. If they weren't, the vehicle was probably the commo car, keeping the gypsies in touch with their unlikely boss back in Okie City.

The mounted M-60s were too high to raise much dust, but McKay could see the muzzle flames stabbing for him like spears. The vehicle seemed to be getting awfully close, and so were the heavy-jacketed bullets splintering the trees and kicking gouges in the hard-packed earth all around him. A feeling of helplessness squatted like a hippo on his shoulders; his MP5 was worth nothing past two hundred meters, and the bullets would just bounce off the improvised armor.

McKay wasn't a nervous type, but the situation wasn't making him real comfortable; nothing about Guardians training made you bulletproof. He wet his lips to keep from saying "What the hell are you waiting for, Sloan? Tire marks on your tongue?"

As if Sloan were reading his mind, McKay heard the *chunk!* of the M-203 launcher. Then he came all over worried that Sloan had fired prematurely. The forty mike-mikes had an outside range around four hundred meters. A short round would probably be enough to make the armored vehicle stand off and shoot them to pieces.

A spiky white flash stabbed off the front glacis of the improvised armored car. A heartbeat later McKay heard the welcome, high-pitched crack of a shaped-charge head. Sam had dropped a high-explosive, dual-purpose round with his customary precision.

The carryall zigzagged briefly but never went out of control. The gunner up top quit shooting and vanished from view. With any luck he'd had a hind leg or two vaporized by a jet of incandescent copper.

The gypsies uttered furious screams. Some of them started firing weapons full-auto over their handlebars. *That's it, scum suckers, keep it up*, McKay thought. *Keep burning that ammo.*

He drew down on a man with a plastic toy Viking helmet on his head, squeezed off a single round as the gypsies crossed two hundred meters. He missed. It was definitely turning out to be one of those days.

The motorized line was spreading as it thundered forward, fanning out to flank the defenders. A dry irrigation ditch ran south of the house, making an *L* with the windbreak trees on Casey's end, its banks elevated just shy of a meter above the surrounding ground, which was a break. On the other hand, an erosion-rutted dirt road ran down to the house from the north at McKay's end, which was no help at all.

McKay took another shot at the plastic Viking, spilled his ass in some kind of ugly, low bush. Score one for the good guys. Another shot from Sloan's launcher floated a bit, struck the lip of the armored carryall's upper decks in a cascade of blinding sparks.

"Drat," Sloan said.

"'Drat?'" McKay echoed. He thumbed the selector switch to auto. He wanted to be able to pulse quick three-round bursts at the riders, trying to flank as they began to show apparent lateral motion. He had a light enough finger on the trigger to squeeze single shots into the targets coming straight at him.

He kept an eye peeled for the dude in the tinfoil suit. He didn't find him. With luck, Case had managed to drop him.

More likely he was keeping back inside the huge cloud of yellow dust the bikers and carryall were kicking up.

As fit their usual balls-out macho style, the gypsies were leading off with a direct assault. That kind of full-frontal exposure would've cost them the whole thing then and there if McKay had had his Maremont.

As it was, it did serve to maximize casualties. With the ground-combat instincts even the skeptical McKay had to admit he was developing, Sloan shifted fire to pop a white phosphorus round a hundred yards in front of their improvised battle line. The white starfish unfolded almost under the front tire of a bike with a metal fairing shaped like a demon's mask. It fell over and exploded. Possibly stunned or killed by the blast, the rider fried without a peep.

Not so his buddies. The road gypsies were charging all in a mass, like medieval cavalry. It wasn't quite as crazy as it sounded. Given their reputation for ferocity—not to mention atrocity—it took a lot of balls for your basic sodbuster, even armed with a magazine rifle, to stand against a concentrated road gypsy charge. All those exotically chopped bikes with their flamboyant riders pounding down on you en masse tended to jelly your guts for true.

If you weren't used to even worse. The Guardians weren't incapable of fear, and wouldn't have been selected for the job if they were; fear is one of Man's most useful emotions, if properly controlled. And control it they did. The road gypsies scared them, but fell far short of freaking them out.

Four other bikes caught the best of the blast of phosphorus flakes. Two riders fell screaming, covered by flakes of metal that burned hot enough to cut through steel and clung like army ants. A third roared straight ahead, unheeding, streaming thin tendrils of smoke from the black leather outfit that covered him from crown to boot soles. Another seemed unaffected, but apparently phosphorus flecks had hit his gas tank; he rolled on for forty meters, firing an M16 between his upswept handlebars, and then the tank blew in a huge blossom of yellow fire that propelled him forward like a stuntman shot from a circus cannon. The exploding gasoline engulfed another rider, who rode, screaming and burning, straight toward the trees until Sloan put a burst into him from his Galil.

The remaining gypsies faltered fifty meters from the trees. Several pressed forward, one swinging a spiked iron ball on a long chain. McKay shot him, Sloan another, and Levy dropped the last five meters from the trees with two shots from the Python.

And then the road gypsies were straggling back toward the gap the carryall had made in the wire. Levy cheered hoarsely. McKay allowed himself a grin.

And then another line of motorcycles appeared on the skyline, black as death on blue.

CHAPTER
ELEVEN ————————————————————

"Sabotage," the man in the black jumpsuit said in a quiet hiss, "is a most serious matter."

The words fell flat and anechoic in the main suit locker. The unoccupied suits stood whitely mute all around like a funeral cortege of Pillsbury Dough Boys.

The black jumpsuits of the Safety Oversight men ranged to either side of the chamber from the entryway to the lock, held fast to the deck by magnets in the soles of their slippers so they appeared to be standing at ease in normal gravity, made them suitable attendants for a funeral. For a death, anyway.

"Most serious, Doctor," Mallory agreed, giving the title only the slightest sarcastic lilt. The orbital station's administrative head spoke English as a second language. His grasp of the tongue's nuance was tentative enough to permit Mallory a touch of whistling past the graveyard.

The huge flat face nodded. Space had turned its owner into an odd creature, indeed. The face had begun clay-colored, with brutal, blunt cheekbones and a mashed-looking nose, eyes black chips of glass with pronounced epicanthic folds shrouding the corners, crowned by stiff black hair. The migration of bodily fluids upward had inflated it into a parody of Yellow Peril: Genghis Khan's acromegalic idiot executioner, his distorted body too small for that giant face, floating in midair.

But this Mongoloid's no idiot, ridiculous though his pretensions to the title of scientist *are,* Mallory reflected. Hocevar Milos was many unpleasant things, but stupid wasn't one of them.

"It pleases me to see you so concerned, Doctor," Hocevar hissed. "What you have been brought here to witness will therefore surely gratify your sense of justice as well as outrage you—in the name of the great work we are called here to accomplish, of course."

He turned and nodded to his men. One of them knocked on the hatch at the far end of the compartment from the air lock. Mallory felt his heart begin a free-fall of premonition as the hatch swung open.

"We have identified the party responsible for the aborting of our attempt to liquidate the madman Iskander Bey," Hocevar intoned. "In the interests of the Federated States of Europe and all mankind, we have determined to take decisive action. As a humanitarian, you approve this speed of action, yes?"

Two men in black jumpsuits stepped through the hatch, pulling a figure in a white jumpsuit between them. Her feet did not touch the deck. Her long blond hair hung in her face.

Mallory's heart reversed and jumped into his throat. Sylvie!

But no—her skin tone was wrong, a touch too strawberry, and the hair was too long. The captive raised her head.

He barely recognized Angela Hughes, the British-born assistant optical systems engineer. Her once pretty face was mottled purple and green and swollen almost past recognition.

"She required encouragement to confess," Hocevar said softly in Mallory's ear. "You'll be pleased to know we have it all on videotape."

Is his voice heavier with insinuation than usual? Mallory wondered with a wildness he hoped didn't show in his face. *He* was the one who had sabotaged the Cygnus laser. Did the Hungarian truly not know, or was he simply toying with him?

Other scientists and technicians were entering the suit locker now, not captives of the Safety Oversight men but distinctly being herded by them: Parker, the black American physicist; Sanjitay of India, who like his Italian colleague, Macchio, standing sullenly beside him with a lock of russet hair falling in his foxy narrow face, had been working at CERN before the One-Day War; Mitchell and Krieger and Sejnowsky. And, of course, Sylvie Braestrop. Some of them looked resentful. Sylvie looked afraid.

"You will observe, Dr. Mallory," Hocevar said, raising his voice slightly, "that we have gathered the most important personnel together here. The rest"—he gestured toward glass-eyed pickups installed around the compartment—"are witnessing these proceedings via video monitors.

"Ladies and gentlemen of Cygnus," he continued, "we see before us a traitor. Someone who has committed gross treason not simply against Yevgeny Maximov, chairman by the consent of all peoples of the Federated States of Europe, but against us all. Against every one of us, not just her comrades and friends but against all humanity.

"It lies within our power to unify our strife-torn planet, by turning an evil implement devised by the nation that remains the single greatest barrier to unification back upon its creator. This woman, Angela Hughes, sought to stand in the way. Is it not appropriate, then, that now, with the device restored and prepared to render its greatest service, she shall pay the price of her betrayal?"

"What about a trial?" Krieger asked, his English thickly brushed with a German accent.

Hocevar smiled. It made him resemble an Easter Island head even more exactly, Mallory thought. "We are about establishing a new world order, based upon scientific principles—a goal with which you have every one expressed yourselves in accord. We know the truth. We propose to act upon it without delay."

The inner door of the air lock slid open with a slight pop as the seal broke.

Hughes was marched forward. Next to Mallory she hung back, and her sea-green eyes met his. They were full of pain, and something else. She opened her bruised and puffy lips as if to speak, but the black jumpsuits hustled her on toward the open door.

Just short of the lock, her captors stopped and grabbed the shoulders of her suit. Obviously it had been retailored for the occasion; it fell open at once, as if secured with Velcro. Her body was surprisingly lush and well formed, Mallory thought, her complexion peaches-and-cream. Really classic English, and the bruises and marks of a cigarette end—or soldering iron, perhaps—had been applied with perverse and exquisite care so as not to deface its beauty too greatly.

She came out of it, then, began to fight. As impassive as Pacific idols, the Safety Oversight men lifted her so her bare feet flailed uselessly, propelled her into the lock. She hit the outboard hatch with a thump, launched herself outward with an agility that belied her docility of moments before.

The hatch slammed in her face.

She beat on the armored glass port with tiny, futile fists. Hocevar nodded, and a flat-screen set beside the lock glowed alive, windowed to show one view from inside the lock and another from the other side of the hull. The stars looked far and cold.

"Observe," Hocevar said, "as we consign the traitor to the mercy of outer space, in full view of the Earth she betrayed."

"No, no! Please, God, *no!*" The cries came muffled through the thick hatch as they spilled forth full volume from the monitor's speakers. *"Nooo!"*

The outer hatch opened behind her. The cries vanished in a puff of outward-rushing air.

The force of air exploding into vacuum blew Angela Hughes out of the lock.

Sylvie Braestrop sobbed and clutched Mallory's arm. He heard the intake of Sanjitay's breath, and Krieger's muttered *"Scheisse."*

You didn't explode in a vacuum; explosive decompression was a B-movie myth. But the air was sucked out of your lungs in a midwinter's-day cloud of condensed moisture, and your skin began to bloom with a false pink glow of health as capillaries ruptured beneath the surface. He had heard you lost consciousness at once—from the sudden cold, he thought.

He hoped to God it was true. That final scream would ring in his ears forever.

Angela Hughes still seemed to be kicking as she tumbled away from the station, a pale, naked frog falling alone into the dark, her final frenzy contrasting with the wedge of Earth, blue-and-white serene, that filled the lower right corner of the monitor.

Mallory put his arm around his assistant, hugged her close.

So where the hell is Tommy? McKay wondered as the reinforced road gypsies came sweeping back in a line that stretched to encircle them like Plastic Man's arms. The former Green Beanie and Stubbs had gotten away from the Herk okay, but there were any number of things that could have gone wrong: a chute failing to deploy, a hard-luck landing to break a leg on a hidden rock, a worse-luck—worst of all *possible* luck, more likely—landing right in among the road gypsies. McKay had almost unlimited faith in Rogers's abilities, but sometimes a stray chunk of metal just whistled in and took you behind the ear no matter what kind of stone superman you happened to be.

The Guardians did tend to be lucky, he could console himself—however you happened to define luck. Maybe they made it themselves. One way or another, Tommy stood a better chance of pulling through than almost anybody.

Including, at this point in time, his buddies. Tactically speaking, they were fucked. Just four guys who didn't have a lot of ammunition but who did have a whole lot of people who wanted them dead. Preferably slowly.

He checked one of their three precious claymores, which lay beside him, behind the lip of the irrigation trench that ran along the treeline. The cap was in place, the electrical hand detonator—called a clacker for the noise it made, just before *boom*—connected by a cord on a nifty automatic takeup reel like a tape measure. It was a great little device for wreaking grief on the enemy when they tried to come over the wire. Too bad they didn't *have* any wire.

"Okay, Casey," he ordered, "go for it. You too, Levy." He had to raise his voice to make the flight crewman hear him above the rising engine scream. Fortunately, as an ex-Parris Island drill instructor, he had a certain knack for that kind of thing.

"You sure you're up to it?" he bellowed at the flight crew-man. What *it* was, was fading back to the long-looted and weather-silvered toolshed southwest of the sunken farmhouse to help hold the perimeter with the M16 and about four mags worth of ammo he'd recovered from the seven gypsies they'd splashed within fifty meters of their position. McKay had offered Levy the option of diving into the house and popping up and down like a militant prairie dog to fire up the bad guys when and as. After all, he wasn't a Guardian. You couldn't expect *him* to be a hard-core hero.

"I'm sure as hell going to try," called back Levy, already in motion. "I've heard about what these happy campers do to their captives."

No sooner did Casey pull for the derelict henhouse on the northwest corner of their irregular perimeter, lugging an Ingram machine pistol Levy had scarfed for him, along with his rifle and his enormous Dirty Harry Magnum in its shoulder holster, than the dude with the tassels and the whole-body mirror shades popped his bike up out of whatever draw he'd run it into. Not *all* road gypsies were just frothing with eagerness to run right up the barrel of a gun. *This* shrewd weenie had ducked under cover and let his loyal troopies gather intelligence for him on the defenders' deployments and firepower. Pathetic as *those* were.

McKay did what he could with precisely metered bursts and single shots, dropping three attackers into the fallow fields. At least there was no more heavy chopper fire raking the trees. Things had gotten scaly all at once, so McKay wasn't sure whether Sloan had put another one into the field-expedient armored car or whether one of the earlier hits had made the puppy brew up, as they used to say in the North African desert half a century before McKay pulled his time there. It was burning with a real satisfactory amount of dancing orange flame—and a humongous pillar of black, black smoke that was going to draw unattached bad guys from all over the Staked Plains.

The north arm of the pincers started to close in on the defenders. A burly, red-bearded biker with one side of his head shaved and the other dyed magenta came booming down the road firing a Uzi across his chest. McKay heard the thump of Sloan's grenade launcher, followed instantly by the popping rattle of his Galil.

Dirt flung by a near miss stung McKay's cheek and filled his left eye with tears as he wheeled to track the bearded biker. Instead of a measured burst, he just had to haul back on the trigger, spraying the road gypsy with all the rest of the bullets in his magazine.

The bearded man bellowed agony and laid his bike down. It spun in the dirt as it hurtled forward and crashed into an upright holding up the tin roof of an open one-vehicle shelter like a detached carport.

Blinking frantically to clear his eye, McKay dropped the mag, crammed another into the H&K's well. Engine noise was rolling over him like Malibu breakers; when he raised his head, there were five bikes bearing down on him from the east in a wedge, riders brandishing spiked clubs and chains and what he would have sworn was an honest-to-God broadsword.

He reared back, bringing the MP5 to bear from his hip. This was no time for subtlety, especially since he saw one thick arm trying to hold the twin conduits of a sawed-off side-by-side shotgun right in his personal direction.

He held back the trigger, sweeping the machine pistol from left to right, hoping like hell the H&K wouldn't misfeed; the trouble with your vaunted German engineering was that it was *too* precise, leaving no margin for error—or abuse. The special-issue MP5s were meant to be murder weapons pure and simple, used in quick in-and-out commando-style actions, not Old West goddam shootouts on the Great Plains.

A skinny son of a bitch with his chest painted to match three electric-blue spikes of hair sticking from his shaven head went down, then a rider who was faceless in a leather mask. Finally a thick .45-caliber slug found the tattooed biceps of the man with the shotgun; the double barrels twitched aside and blasted into the side of the man in the mask, who seemed to be holding it together despite a round in the shoulder. The double-ought cracked his rib cage open and he spilled.

The shotgunner fell over. The two intact road gypsies who'd come in with him decided discretion was the better part of ballsiness and spun around, raising a wake of tan earth as they boogied.

The motorcycle's forward momentum carried it ahead on its side, right straight for McKay. He threw himself to the side, tucked and rolled as the front wheel hit the tree he'd been sheltering next to and ground over the faint imprint his big body had made in the low embankment.

Slick as Mikhail Baryshnikov at a Wesson Oil party, McKay came right on up on one knee with his machine pistol's butt snugged neatly to his shoulder. He lined up the battle sights on the shotgunner, who wore outrageous black-and-red makeup over a clown-white base that had gotten all runny with heat and dust and made him look like Ozzy Osbourne having a bad period, and who had managed not to get a thigh-booted leg mangled when he dropped his chopper. McKay pulled the trigger.

Click.

CHAPTER
TWELVE ————————————————

He knew what *that* sound meant: the MP5 had jammed, and his dick was in the dirt.

With surprising speed the gypsy with the metal-head makeup whipped a .38 snubby out of somewhere and snapped a left-handed shot at McKay. It chunked into the tree next to his head with an axe blow sound.

"Well, fuck," McKay said. He threw the H&K spinning into the biker's face. The metal butt plate bounced off his forehead with a crack. The gypsy yelled "Shit!" and triggered a wild shot toward the dust-screened sky.

McKay snapped open the Kevlar flap of his holster. The Guardians' combat pistol training had been as exhaustive as every other department, and they had been drilled in the principle that it's the man who gets the first shot on target who almost always wins. That usually meant taking time to brace and aim, however quickly.

But sometimes there was *no time*, like this time, and the training covered that too. He snaked his own .45 out, thumbing off the safety as he poked it toward the biker from the hip as if he were pointing his finger, and fired twice.

One shot kicked up dirt beside a thigh-high jackboot. The other hit the biker in the nuts and doubled him over in a howling knot of pain.

McKay let him wail while he took stock of the situation. The noise was just the sort to get his buddies' minds right as to what it meant to fuck with a Guardian, and anyway was music to McKay's ears.

The situation sucked. Sloan was dueling with a biker about forty yards out, who was cranking at him with some kind of automatic 5.56, a CAR-15 or doctored Mini-14 or whatever the hell. The bad guy was keeping his elaborately Mohawked head well covered behind his fallen cycle. Sloan was obviously unwilling to burn a precious grenade on the bastard.

Tracking on around clockwise, McKay saw Casey blasting away vigorously at gypsies circling the little sad clump of farm buildings like Indians in some old wagon-train movie. At long range Casey could drive nails with that Remington of his, and in the air could practically write his name on enemy planes with the inboard Vulcan. But on the ground at close quarters he was a total write-off. Inside fifty meters, he needed a full-auto shotgun to hit a Winnebago. But he was busting caps enthusiastically enough to make the bad guys keep their distance, at any rate.

Swiveling his head the other way on his bull neck, McKay was just in time to see Levy stumble back out of his crouch behind the toolshed. McKay thought he'd caught one in the hip—

—but just then, out of the corner of his eye, McKay saw six or eight road gypsies pouring right up the road, not forty meters out, choppers howling on full throttle.

All of a sudden his combat-modified Colt side arm seemed awful puny. There was only one thing to do.

"Sam!" he screamed. *"Forward roll!"*

There was no time to wait for acknowledgment, no time to do more than hope Sloan heard and that the puke he was shooting it out with didn't have any marksmanship merit badges of his own. He jammed the .45 back in his holster, scooped up the claymore and the detonator, and dived into the road.

At least one of the charging road gypsies had a 9-mm submachine gun and was firing it over his handlebars. McKay could tell by the sound of the gunshots kicking up spurts of dirt around his ankles. He threw himself into a dive, planted the short legs of the mine in the hardpan of the yard, with the embossed legend FRONT TOWARD ENEMY aimed right at the gypsies' front wheels.

He rolled two meters away from the mine, winding up on his belly. He thumbed open the clacker's cover, buried his face in his arms, and *squeezed*.

The molded plastic of the claymore was a highly directional explosive. It sent a nasty spike of shock and incandescent gas straight back—more or less toward where Sam had been squaring off with his own personal member of Forrie's Second Finest—and a steadily expanding fan of *much nastier* steel marbles right into the road gypsies' faces.

A tsunami of hot air rolled over McKay, and the roar of the claymore exploding bulged in his eardrums in spite of the semipermanent plugs the Guardians wore. It was the sort of noise to give you religion, the kind where once you heard it, all you wanted to do was lie there and maybe become real small so no one would ever find you again. Even when the bang was on *your* side.

But Billy McKay was going to stay six-three no matter how hard he wished otherwise, and since he still had sphincter control, he figured to be holding steady at 225. He raised his head.

There were parts of bikes and bikers strewn all over the road. Drawing his pistol again, he got to his feet. This was a satisfying sight. *Something* had gone right today.

''McKay!'' Sam Sloan's voice shouted, simultaneously inside and outside his head.

There is a basic law of the grunt in combat: when it doubt, *drop*. It was a lesson he'd learned over and over again in the Med with Force RECON and SOG-SWAC, and nothing he'd seen or lived through as boss Guardian gave him the slightest reason to doubt it. But when he heard Sam's warning shout, he just turned around flat-footed. After all, he had a .45 in his fist.

Which did him no fucking good at all. A Harley swept by. A big silvery arm stuck out from it and caught right under the collarbone and just plain clotheslined him.

He went flying back ass over crew cut. His Colt was knocked out of his hand and went somewhere else. So did his wind.

Having fucked up big-time, he remembered he was a Guardian in midair, tucked himself into a ball, dropped his shoulder, rolled on contact, and managed to come up onto first knees and then feet, precisely as if that's what he meant to do all the time, and, aside from a little bit of wobble, managing not to show that he felt as if he'd been hit by Jose Canseco with a forty-ounce bat.

But it wasn't the aging Yankee slugger who'd nailed him. It was the jerk in the shiny clown suit, who was pivoting his big bike around one leg that seemed, like all the rest of him, to be encased in fucking *armor*.

No wonder my damn chest hurts, McKay thought. From nearby he heard shots, the crack of a grenade, engines howling, and men screaming in anger and pain and for the general hell of it. The man in the suit of armor held his undivided attention as he dropped the stand and swung off his hog. What looked like white horse tails bounced from his massive metal-clad shoulders as he advanced on McKay with an evil smile on his face.

He was at least an inch taller than McKay and, even accounting for his outfit, seemed broader. He had a huge moon face with a fringe of red-gold beard. His eyes were green, slightly slanted, rimmed with red. His nose was mashed onto his face to a considerable extent, and he had one gold tooth and one missing from the grin he gave his intended victim. For a road gypsy he was astonishingly normal-looking, if you overlooked the iron long johns.

From the sound of things McKay figured the gypsies were still circling the ranch buildings firing up his buddies. He didn't know whether they were going to be content to let their boss deal with McKay, but he didn't have time to sweat it as the man snaked a weighted chain from around his waist and began twirling it as he stalked toward McKay.

McKay pulled his Kabar from its sheath on the left breast of the jumpsuit. Unless that outfit was plastic covered with shiny mylar—and his sternum didn't feel like it was—he wasn't sure what good he was going to be able to do with a knife. Maybe he could cut the bastard's throat.

The mental debate got suddenly settled when Iron Man wrapped his chain around the Kabar's blade and twitched it right out of McKay's hand, which hadn't got all the strength of its grip back since he'd busted a knuckle of it on one of William Morrigan's merry men.

"Well, *fuck*," McKay said, and lunged at the man. The armored gypsy was wide open. McKay laid his forehead open tackling him around the waist, and they both went down with a sound like a Maytag falling out a window.

They rolled over and over in the dust and faded paper debris of the ranch-house yard. The plate armor seriously restricted the road gypsy's mobility, but also seriously restricted what McKay could *do* to him. After an interval of grunting, confused flailing, McKay wound up astride his steel-plated chest, got two good shots into his face and knocked out at least another tooth before the gypsy leader caught him on the side of his head with a roundhouse.

McKay's head went *clank,* and he toppled over, seeing flash bulbs go off behind his eyes. The fucker had some kind of jointed steel gloves on. They hurt.

They came to their feet facing each other. The boss gypsy seemed to have lost one of his horse-tail tassels. The fight continued to swirl around them, but the noise seemed to be coming from a million miles away. The gypsies seemed to be keeping their fire clear for fear of putting one in their maximum man. If they didn't keep that up, there wasn't much McKay could do about it.

He tried to close again, got a surprisingly quick metal jab for his pains. He jerked his head aside at the last possible millisecond, and the gauntlet sliced his left cheek open along the bone as cleanly as a razor.

He ducked a left-handed follow-up shot, rammed a shoulder into the armored midriff again. Instead of trying to carry forward and bring his opponent down again, this time he straightened at once as soon as he had the bastard's weight back on his heels, put a right and left of his own into the biker's face, turning it into a demon mask of blood.

The biker leader went to one knee, head wagging like a fighting bull about to drop. *Gotcha*, McKay thought, and started a kick for the bearded point of the jaw that would snap the puke's neck clean no matter how thickly muscled it was.

And a gypsy skidded his chopper up behind him in a welter of dust and clipped him on the back of his head with a rifle butt. It wasn't a nylon stock made by Mattel, either; it was good wood and steel.

McKay's lights flickered. A head shot generally didn't put you all the way under unless it poked in a corner of your skull so you'd stay there for good. But more fireworks ricocheted around the inside of McKay's cranium, and his stomach started doing slow rolls.

He was on his knees, with the steel knuckles on the boss gypsy's gauntlets digging into his chin as he throttled him. McKay grabbed the wrists. They felt like pipes. They might have been welded in place for all the effect he had on them.

His vision was starting to go black all over again, and there was an ugly, thin mosquito singing in his ears that he didn't think was too good a sign. With his left hand he tried to get purchase on the gypsy's little finger to break it while his right slammed short, savage punches to the side of the man's head.

Even on short punches McKay could manage quite a few foot-pounds; he could buckle a cinder block with a six-incher. But the gypsy just let his head rock on its enormous neck and kept on smiling through the blood, so that his remaining teeth were like moons shining through crimson clouds.

Billy McKay had about run out of altitude, airspeed, and ideas, as Casey put it from time to time. He was also just about out of oxygen. He set his jaw, bulged his neck muscles, and grimly kept slugging.

For a brief flicker of a moment his oxygen-starved brain thought he saw Mike Levy's lean face above the white horse tail hanging from the gypsy's right shoulder, grinning demonically.

And suddenly he was falling on his ass, flung backward by a convulsive motion by the gypsy leader. The armored man opened his mouth and emitted a high-pitched, horrible scream and a spray of blood. He staggered back, hands reaching back over his shoulders, trying to claw at his back.

Completely clueless, McKay scrambled to his feet, looking for weapons. Sure enough, there was Levy, lying on the ground clutching his hip, still grinning like a man getting a blow job.

The armored road gypsy fell onto his back, shrieked a whole octave higher, and just came exploding up off the ground. He spun around twice and fell into the open doorway of the gutted farmhouse.

About that moment McKay's hand found what a throbbing bruise on his hip had been trying to remind him of: the fat, tapered cylinder of a white phosphorus grenade. He ripped it off his belt, tore out the pin, and tossed it down the hole.

There was a boom, and a gout of thick white smoke vomited out of the ground. The ugly burned-hair aroma that McKay had been belatedly becoming aware of suddenly got a whole lot worse. The screaming abruptly stopped.

Concussion must have taken him out before the phosphorus had a chance to go to work on him, he thought. *Son of a bitch.*

''McKay!''

It was Levy's voice this time. *I'm getting to old for this shit,* McKay thought wearily. But he wasn't getting caught standing a second time. He dropped.

Something slammed his ribs like a sledgehammer, spinning him in midair. He landed on his back, blinking and gasping with pain.

A bearded gypsy on a bike was laughing at him from behind round-lensed glasses and a Dirty Harry horse pistol aimed right for the bridge of his nose.

CHAPTER
THIRTEEN

McKay sighed. It was definitely shaping up to be one of those days.

For form's sake he got ready to throw himself to the side. The Kevlar vest he wore under his coveralls had stopped a glancing round from punching through him, though his long-suffering rib cage had absorbed the bullet's force. A solid hit from a .44 Mag would probably go right through him—or drive an icicle of stretched-out Kevlar deep into his innards, which would do him no good.

The knuckle whitened as the bearded man's trigger finger tightened.

There was a *splutch* sound and a hole popped open in the road gypsy's black leather jacket between his left nipple and armpit. His upper torso jackknifed forward across the up-swept bars of the bike.

Flame bloomed from the .44's muzzle. McKay felt the wind of the fat bullet's passage hot on the side of his head. Even as the aftermath of the Magnum's roar was ringing inside his head he heard a faint but solid thud, like an echo of the gunshot. No echo; a big caliber rifle report from far away. Somebody was sniping.

The bike's engine roared and it jackrabbited away, the bearded gypsy hunched over the bars but still seemingly in control.

From the distance came the sewing-machine pops of a 5.56 weapon firing full automatic. It was a little too quick and persistent to be an M16 or other assault rifle. McKay's instincts identified it almost at once: somebody had gotten to the sidecar-mounted M-249 Squad Automatic Weapon whose operators they'd taken out in the opening moments of the fight.

"Great," McKay muttered, "just great." God was messing with them, tantalizing them by rescuing them from one doom only to lay another on them just as they thought things were okay. God as Brian de Palma; *great*.

As he got up on all fours to scramble for cover—he wasn't going into the house for fucking *anything* since that Willy Peter went off—he noticed that the road gypsies circling the yard were beginning to peel away and ride off across the khaki landscape at a great rate. Even as he watched, one threw both hands in the air and spilled off his cycle as a burst of machine-gun fire kicked up dirt around him.

He dropped flat on his belly to take stock of the situation. The road gypsies were definitely bugging out as fast as they could. Sam Sloan came popping up out of the deeper irrigation ditch that ran along the south side of the yard, where he'd gotten pinned down after being flushed by the back blast of McKay's claymore—and did his part to keep them headed in the right direction by furiously busting caps after them. Remembering his earlier theological reflections, he felt almost a sense of anticlimax: *What shaft are we due for* this *time?*

He came up to one knee, looking cautiously around. Casey Wilson was sticking his head cautiously out of the henhouse, holding his rifle ready at the hip, like he was really going to be able to do anything with it if the bad guys were inside half a klick. There were a lot of road gypsies and bikes lying around, and a greasy, thick gray smoke hanging in air that stung the eyes and throat and smelled unbelievably foul.

There was somebody's abandoned Mini-14 lying about ten meters away. McKay duckwalked to it, picked it up, checked to make sure there were rounds in the magazine. Feeling more secure, he went over to check Levy.

Levy wasn't looking quite so chipper anymore. His face was pale and clammy, blue lips peeled back from his gums. As he knelt beside him McKay said, "What the fuck did you do to that asshole?"

Levy managed a laugh. "My M16 jammed and I ran out of bullets for that tin-plated pimp gun of Sloan's. Then I got hit. When I got things sorted out, I noticed you waltzing with your little friend. Nobody was paying any attention to me, and you didn't seem to be doing so well, so I thought it was time for the heroic Military Airlift Command to take a hand."

McKay was trying to tear open the tough and blood-soaked fabric of Levy's trousers and not doing a very good job. Belatedly it occurred to him he'd make more headway if he took the time to hunt down his knife.

"So what'd you *do*?" he persisted.

"We're supposed to carry survival kits in pockets on our pants legs. I may not have been carrying my side arm, but I had *that*. So I decided to see what would happen if I poked a live flare down the back of Bunky's neck."

He shook his head. "The results were everything I could have hoped for. *Whoa,* that hurts."

McKay backed off, assuming the aircrewman was talking about his own ministrations and not the road gypsy's encounter with the flare. He already knew Levy was a mess, not that bullet wounds were ever real minor. Time to go for the knife and see how much first-aid gear had survived the airplane ride and the day's other amusements. He had Guardians training in wound treatment, too, but Tommy was the unit medic. If only he were here. . . .

"*Billy,*" Casey's voice said in his mastoid speaker. "*We've got more company, man. Bikes, bearing o-eight-five.*"

McKay looked up. Two cycles were rolling across the field,

swerving from time to time to avoid a sprawled body or a crater left by Sloan's vest-pocket artillery.

"Well, fuck, Casey, can't you just kill them? They're far enough away that you oughta be able to hit 'em."

"Hold your fire, McKay," a calm, familiar, and oh-so-welcome voice said in the back of McKay's head. *"It's Tom. I brought some friends."*

"Where's Stubbs?" McKay asked as the two bikes pulled up in the yard. Two guys were doubled up on one, and Tom rode behind the other's driver. None of them was the Hercules' navigator.

"I think he caught the tail plane coming out, Billy. His chute never deployed."

Levy moaned.

"Who are these people?" McKay asked.

Tom dismounted and walked toward Levy and McKay, naturally gravitating toward a wounded man. It always struck McKay as strange how a complete killing machine like Tommy could turn into such a mother hen when he played medic.

"Indiges."

Indiges meant "indigenous personnel," which was Special Forces talk for "locals."

"I can *see* that, Tom," McKay said with exaggerated clarity.

He decided he desperately needed a smoke. He reached to his breast pocket only to discover a couple of cigar-shaped cellophane packages of tobacco crumbles. Going mano a mano with some goon in full armor wasn't a recommended way of preserving your finer imported cigars.

"Fuck," he said with feeling, "fuck, fuck, fuck, fuck, *fuck.*"

"Billy, this is Skids Rodey," Tom said as he knelt next to Levy, nodding to the driver of the first cycle. When they were approaching, McKay had figured him for some kind of Plains Indian. He had straight black hair that hung to his shoulders, a dark, round face, and, to complete the impression, wore what before the war would've been ten years or ten thousand dollars in the form of an eagle feather stuck crosswise through his hair at the back of his head.

Up close he didn't look quite so Indian, though he had the stocky kind of build, low-slung and heavy in chest and shoulders, that McKay associated with Kiowas he'd known in the service. As a matter of fact, he looked a whole lot like Dan Aykroyd crossed with John Belushi. He grinned and stuck out his hand.

"Hey, I'm pleased to meet you," he said as McKay shook it. He had on a wide, bronze-looking armlet and a black Def Leppard T-shirt.

In his free hand he carried a big long lever-action rifle with a magazine and a scope: a .30-06 Winchester Model 1895, a real Teddy Roosevelt Deer-Slaughtering Special. "He took care of the man holding the pistol on you, Billy," Tom said, expertly slicing open Levy's trousers with his own knife. Tom Rogers never lost *his* knife.

McKay looked at him with new interest. He was carrying a bit more of a gut than McKay liked to see, but he looked solid. Also, he'd saved McKay's ass, which definitely gave him a leg up toward being classed as "good troop."

"Thanks, man," McKay said. "Appreciate it."

Rodey shrugged and gave his head an embarrassed little shake. "It was my pleasure."

"Yeah," his partner said. "He's been gunning for that bearded guy for years."

"This is Scooter Trash, Billy," Tom said.

This one was tall, a hair taller than McKay, and a touch on the gawky side. Like his buddy, he looked to be in his early twenties. With a pair of Erwin Rommel Afrika Korps goggles pushed up on his mop of bushy light brown hair, he bore a passing resemblance to a young Bruce Springsteen playing Jimmy Dean playing a biker. He had on dusty Levi's, a tan jacket, and an AK-47 on an Israeli-style sling hung around his neck.

McKay stuck out his hand. "Pleased to . . . say *what*?"

"I'm Scooter," the kid said. "Scooter Trash."

McKay held back his hand. "Is that the name on your birth certificate?"

"Say, these men just saved our lives, McKay," said Sloan, who'd come wandering over, holding his Galil-203 combo warily and keeping a general eye out for trouble.

"Yeah? Well, in case you ain't been keeping up on current events, I've had kind of a rough day, Navy boy, and I'm in a real mood to get some *answers*."

Sloan gave them his patented, *don't mind him, he's an asshole, but he's our asshole* look. Rodey mugged and wagged his eyebrows. Scooter gave a relaxed kind of laugh.

"My family caught it in the war," he said easily. "That's what I call myself now. I don't think it much matters what I used to be called."

"No, I guess not." McKay shook his hand, giving Sloan his own *I know I'm an asshole, and up yours, anyway, Navy boy* glare past his shoulders.

"Who's your other friend?" Sloan asked, all folksy James Garner, ignoring McKay.

The black-clad driver of the other cycle had been unstrapping the captured SAW from the bike's handlebars, and now swung a long leg off the machine and started over. The M-249 had a box magazine in it at the moment, instead of a belt.

Five meters away, a road gypsy casualty rolled onto his side, pulling a Luger out of a shoulder holster. Sam shouted a warning, started to swing the Galil around.

The rider pivoted and fired a short burst from the hip. Head chunks flew from the gypsy, skull and brains and juice. He rolled over twice and lay twitching. The rider watched a moment more, weapon trained, then resumed walking toward the others.

"Christ," McKay said, "how come we never meet any girls who aren't butch?"

"Allow me to introduce our good friend and associate," Skids Rodey said, after he stopped wincing. "Killer."

"Killer," McKay repeated in disgust.

She arched an eyebrow at him. She was long and lean, maybe an inch short of six feet. Her hair was long and black and hung in a ponytail down her back. Her eyes were blue, her nose kind of snubbed. Her jeans were tight, as was her

black Harley T-shirt, and McKay had to admit to himself he
didn't mind either fact. Her eyebrow was well designed for
arching.

"I'm pleased to meet you, ma'am," Sam Sloan said, maybe
hitting the *I'm* a bit harder than strictly necessary. He took
her hand, bowed slightly, and kissed it.

She grabbed the hair at the back of his head, bent him
back, leaned over him and kissed him hard.

When she let him go he straightened up and stood blinking
and looking a lot more disheveled than a mere firefight had
left him. Killer went over, put a friendly and proprietary arm
around Scooter's shoulders and tousled his hair.

"It's always a pleasure to meet a *real* gentleman," she said
in a whiskey contralto.

Casey turned up and everybody got introduced to everybody else. "Where did you find these people?" McKay asked
the former Green Beret, who was cleaning Levy's wound with
water from a bottle from Skids's Kawasaki.

"They're militia from Clayton. There's a big firefight going
on east of here between the locals and the road gypsies."

"That must've been the smoke we saw just before the *Pig*
blew," Levy said, trying to sit up.

"Take it easy, guy," Rodey said. "Should you be doing
that?"

"Takes my mind off what *he's* doing," Levy said, nodding
at Rogers.

"You sound like you're familiar with this bunch," McKay
said to Rodey, Trash having wandered off to make sure the
other deaders stayed that way.

Rodey nodded. "Heck, yeah. We *knew* some of them, back
before the war."

McKay traded glances with Sloan and started wishing he'd
hunted up his .45 instead of dicking around with Levy. He
knew these were supposed to be good guys, but still . . .

"Renegade SCA types from the Texas–New Mexico area.
Real assholes. Started palling around with the road gypsies
even before, like, the world blew up and everything."

"SCA?"

"Society for Creative Anachronism, Billy," Casey said. "I used to—"

"I know you used to, Casey. We ran into some of your old SCA buddies back in California, among all the other assorted fruits, nuts, and vegetables."

"You've got us pretty well pegged," Rodey said with a laugh. "Say, you really did a job on the Evil Truck of Marcus the Mad."

"Say what?" McKay said again, not really sure he wanted an explanation.

Rodey jerked his head back at the churned-up field. "The homemade armored car out there. The one causing all the air pollution."

"Yeah. Who's Marcus the Mad?"

"He's the leader of this particular pack of scumwads. Big sucker, kind of a red beard, always wears this silly-looking shiny armor."

"Oh, him. He's—"

"Jesus *Christ*!" Scooter exclaimed from the doorway of the sunken house. "What happened in here? It looks like somebody left a giant Thanksgiving turkey in the oven too long. Smells that way too."

"That's Marcus," McKay said.

Rodey looked back at his buddy, who was stumbling out of the smoke wisps still drifting from the house with a marked green tint to him, then pursed his lips, nodded, and gave McKay a thumbs-up.

Rogers was spraying some artificial skin over Levy's wound, which kept out dirt and germs but let air in. "That's the best I can do right now. Can you ride a motorcycle?"

"Are you kidding, Doc? I couldn't ride one *before* I got shot."

"I meant, can you sit on one? We can strap you down if we have to."

"If I have to, I guess I can manage, if whoever's driving promises to steer around potholes. Do I need to be rushed to Urgent Care or something?"

"You need more than I can give you here," Rogers said, methodically stowing his medic gear, "but the reason I'm asking is that about half the road gypsies in Oklahoma seem to be converging on this spot, and I reckon we'd all stay healthier if we moved."

"Since you put it that way, I think a nice ride in the country's just what I need. What are we waiting for?"

CHAPTER
FOURTEEN ——————————

"There's a story to Scooter's name," Skids Rodey said.

"I'm sure there is," Billy McKay said, morosely turning the bottle in his hands in the light of the kerosene lantern and thinking there was nothing quite so sad as an empty beer bottle. It was the sort of thought he had after he'd emptied a lot of them. "And I suppose you're gonna tell me all about it."

Skids nodded across the heavy oak table in the dining room of the house on the outskirts of Clayton he shared with his partner and Killer, who was Scooter's squeeze—or he was hers, more likely.

"He single-handedly started a revival of Spain Rodríguez' *Trashman* comics before the war," Skids explained. "You know, the one with the big bearded guy who looks kinda like Mr. Zig, who had this humongous machine gun and was always saying stuff like 'Hangdogs of Imperialism, taste leaden death!'"

"Oh, yeah!" Casey exclaimed. He was sitting cross-legged on the bare wood floor in front of the sofa, with his Remington disassembled for cleaning on an ancient edition of *USA Today* fetched from the basement. "I remember those old undergrounds. I think I even, like, saw some of Scooter's stuff, too, now that I think about it. It was pretty cool."

"It figures," McKay said. "You're the one who knows all that commie shit."

He held up two fingers in front of his mouth. Skids fished out a pack of the slim black cigarillos he smoked and poked one at McKay. McKay lit up and reflected that it was a pretty thin diet in comparison to what he was used to. Then again, it was probably a sign he was a degenerate that he'd gotten hooked on Indonesian cigars. Father Perrault had always told him he was a degenerate, back at St. Joe's.

They'd beaten the pursuing gypsies into town that afternoon by a healthy margin. Not that the gypsies had pursued them all that far. An old-timey Country Music Television kind of place on the fringe of the Great Plains, whose architecture ran to Wheat Belt pitch roofs instead of the Mud-Hut Nouveau of most of New Mexico, Clayton had been turning into a ghost town even before the war hit. But the people who stayed were frontier survival types, self-reliant and tough as diner steak, and the days of disorder since the war hadn't made them any more pliable. They had a fair amount of experience dealing with the road gypsies and Reverend Forrie's other elves by now.

Levy was in town at the clinic, where he was in what McKay figured they called serious but stable condition back before the balloon went up. Sam and Tom were out in the front yard trying to find a communications satellite. One of the items that had survived the explosion of the C-130 was their nifty-neat collapsible satlink antenna, which looked like an inside-out tinfoil umbrella. Since a highly directional satellite link didn't suck much power, you could jimmy the Guardians' pocket communicators to talk long-distance with the antenna, but since you had to hold the thing on an unseen target by hand, it was a genuine pain in the ass.

They had successfully linked before sunset, to let Washington know they had survived and to ask what the fuck had happened, aside from that somebody had tried to blow their butts to Jesus. Now they were trying to make their scheduled callback, while Scooter watched. He didn't try to help; neither he nor Skids seemed to be the technical type.

"So that's why he's called Scooter?" McKay asked.

"That's why he calls himself Trash. He's always been called Scooter."

"You're an artist, too, ain't you?"

Rodey grinned and waved a hand at the walls. They were covered with paintings and drawings. They were all well executed, all of women, and most of them nudes, or nearly so.

"You did all these?" McKay asked.

"I did. That's Bunny and Randi and Amber and Khrys and Cat . . ." He paused and sighed, then resumed pointing out pictures with his cigarillo. "And that's T. J., Vaughn, Eve, Annette, Flame . . ."

"Pretty impressive," McKay said. "You dick all of them?"

Rodey raised an eyebrow. Killer snorted and helped herself to a smoke from the pack he'd left on the table.

"So how'd you wind up here?"

"How did a couple of big-city art guys like me and Scoots wind up in this international Mecca of culture? Let me see. Claudia—she was a member of this Leaping Weasel Art Co-op we had back in Albuquerque—Claudia inherited some land from her folks out near Capulin Mountain. She and her husband got into survivalism in the early nineties, like a lot of people. We all sort of played around with it, and then when things really did blow up, we moved out and started our own Art Farm and commune."

"What happened?"

"New Dispensation creeps crawled up their assholes and slit their throats from the inside," said Killer, taking a pull of Stoli from the bottle.

McKay gave her the fish eye. "You're a real sweetheart. Just the type of girl I'd love to take home to Mom."

"She'd be relieved I wasn't a guy."

"After *that*," Skids said loudly, "we became your basic refugees. We wound up essentially being farmhands and handymen."

He opened a fresh bottle of scarfed Michelob and sipped.

"Thought we'd maybe like to try being soldiers of fortune. Go help towns defend themselves, like in *Yojímbo*. That's why we're here; Clayton thought they'd give us a try."

"That means they decided to use them as cannon fodder," Killer offered.

"And what's your part in all this?" McKay asked her.

"Somebody's got to take care of these two."

"Yeah." McKay smirked. "I just *bet* you take care of 'em."

She polished off the last of the vodka, reversed the bottle, and matter-of-factly broke in on the edge of the table. "I don't like your attitude, McKay," she said conversationally.

"Say, does anybody feel like some tamales?" Skids asked. "Mrs. Ramirez from down the road brought us over a tray of them when she heard you'd come to visit—"

The front door opened. A brisk wind blew in Scooter's head. Without his goggles he looked like a sheepdog.

"Sam's got Washington on the line," he said. "They want you."

"I'll just bet they do," McKay said, climbing heavily to his feet, never taking his eye off Killer. She laughed and set the bottle down by the mayonnaise jar she was using as an ashtray.

McKay was still shaking his head and thinking dark thoughts when the duty officer in the White House commo room came on-line.

"We've turned up a few leads in the sabotage of that plane," Washington said. *"They implicate your old friends, the Romans. We expect some arrests shortly."*

"Huh," McKay grunted. It all sounded just too damned pat, not to mention he did not for one little instant believe they were going to be making any busts in the foreseeable future, unless they just planned to roust the first rubble-runners they could get their hooks into. Especially if it really *had* been the CIA renegades who called themselves the Romans who bombed the plane.

"How did they know about our mission?" Sloan asked. All four Guardians were tied into the circuit via their communicators.

They could practically feel the shrug from the other end. *"There's been a lot of stuff in the air lately, if you know what I mean, Commander. The Iskander Bey thing, rumors about Cygnus and Vandenberg, and suddenly the plane that brought you to D.C. is being prepped for a long trip—you know how it is. And our friends in the Company do get paid for knowing how to put two and two together, or used to."*

"Yeah," McKay said, "two and two, my *ass*. What's in the air back there's a stink like week-old shit, my man. It wasn't any God damn accident the gypsies were taking a little road trip into New Mexico today; they were sent out to pick us up if we made it out of the Herkie, and they knew when and where it was gonna blow. Somebody shopped our asses for true."

"Tsk, tsk, McKay. Mustn't get paranoid. I tell you, we—hold on, we're getting a message in from Tide Camp. It's—"

"Oh, my God!"

It was a clear night in Washington, D.C. The bonfires didn't blaze as high among the rice paddies and makeshift buildings around the Tidal Basin as usual. There was some heavy shit going down in the capital. The huge and enigmatic Soong had dedicated himself and Tide Camp to personal loyalty to the president but had scrupulously maintained the Camp's independence from the nearby White House. Whatever was happening now, everybody was glad of the fact.

Meanwhile, nobody felt like silhouetting himself.

There were no fires at all in the park that ran from the Lincoln Memorial to the west end of the Mall. It was Tide Camp's border and buffer. Over the months since the One-Day War, Soong's people had painstakingly tended its grass, which was dutifully coming in green and lush with the spring—and if it was fertilized mainly with human waste, hey, holocaust survivors can't be choosers. The Campers had also carefully fortified it, with razor-tape tangles and trip wires fixed to flares and less friendly items. The process had continued since the president had come back to town—not in spite of his main adviser's vociferous objections to the Camp's continued existence, but largely because of them.

Still, just because the park was meant to be a killzone, if the ax came down, that didn't mean you couldn't kick back and enjoy it on standdown on a warm, still spring evening, as long as you didn't play your box too loud or show any lights bigger than the cigarettes the little group on the steps of the Lincoln Memorial were dragging on.

There were ten of them at the moment, just knocking back some white lightning made by the Armenian enclave out by the Georgetown Reservoir and listening to some Middle Eastern rock 'n' roll. Six Tide Camp troopies, a couple of Filipinas from the Camp, a black girl from one of the allied rubble gangs, and a long, lanky woman in her twenties with hair like a frozen waterfall who was a warlord with the Nuclear Winners. It was your usual Tide Camp party mix.

The Winner woman got up, shook her starburst of pale hair, and started to take off her clothes in time to the music. The partyers stomped and whistled and cheered; this was just the sort of show to completely piss off some of their neighbors. Iron Maggie Connoly and her crew thought it was still the just-say-no eighties. Also, back before the war, the dancer had been one of the top strippers in the greater Washington area.

Wet Willie grinned at his buddy, Ozone, as the dancer, who called herself Horizon, draped a short vest studded with buttons bearing Winner slogans like LICK THE TINS and FUCK AUTHORITY over his prominent ears. He slapped his knees and hooted. He was kind of a string bean, and a notable flake.

"Hey, hey, lookit you," he shrilled. "She put a bag over your head. You gonna get some tonight *fer sure*."

"Not from me, soldier dog," Horizon said, and bopped Willie right in the beak with her round, hard-muscled little ass. He fell over on his back, cracked his skull on the marble steps, and lay there moaning and staring at the stars.

Another troopie frowned and tipped his head to the side. "Hey," he said with a German accent. He was an East German refugee everybody called Matrix after the Arnold character in *Commando*, even though he weighed about sixty kilos soaking wet. "I smell something funny."

Wet Willie screamed.

Everybody turned and looked at him, except Horizon, far gone in her routine. "You being a spaz again?" asked the Gook, a six-foot-two Korean with a Southern California accent.

Wordlessly he pointed upward. A blinding yellow shaft of light was spiking down out of the sky onto the white dome of the Lincoln Memorial.

"We have a paint on the target, Dr. Mallory," Sylvie Braestrop reported breathlessly. "Photometry shows a low scatter coefficient."

"Ah, excellent." Mallory beamed. "The air is clear tonight."

He gazed around the control center at his staff, floating by their consoles in pristine pastel jumpsuits. Out in the middle of it all hung Hocevar like a small, evil black cloud.

Hocevar nodded, almost imperceptibly. Mallory boiled inside: *And what unworthy creature am I, to be taking orders from the likes of you?* He kept his manner composed and cheerful. There was morale to keep up, and anyway, this was a task well worth the doing in spite of that Magyar devil.

"Let's make history, then, shall we? Increase the power output."

Standing side by side on the third-floor promenade above the South Portico of the White House, before the clear plastic sheeting that covered the blown-out windows of the Sun Room, Dr. Marguerite Connoly and Jeffrey MacGregor watched the column of light that shone on the Lincoln Memorial turn from yellow to bluish white. A personal message over a most unexpected channel from no less than Yevgeny Maximov himself had alerted them just moments before.

Shrewd of the chairman to find a way to patch himself over the red phone, MacGregor thought. *He really is a hell of a showman.*

As this show was amply demonstrating. A thunder-crack of sundered air reached the president's ears as a brilliant jet

of stone flash-heated to incandescence fountained into the
night sky.

For some reason MacGregor glanced quickly to the side.
Connoly stood there as if entranced, with the hellish display
doubly reflected in the round lenses of her spectacles. Her
lips were parted, just barely.

"Such *power*," she whispered, unaware that she was heard.

The light and the sound persisted for an eternity of perhaps
ten seconds' duration. Then both stopped, leaving a hole in
the dome whose rim cooled from white to yellow as they
watched and a dazzling purple afterimage line behind
MacGregor's eyes that he thought would never go away as
long as he lived.

His adviser turned to him. "See, Jeffrey?" she said in quiet
triumph. "I told you this Guardian scheme of yours was futile."

He shook himself, as if slowly awakening from deep sleep.
He felt strangely still, like a pond on a still day. But boiling
up beneath that mirror-smooth surface was anger, like a bubble of poison gas welling from a fetid lake bottom.

"That may be," he said. "That may be, but their orders
stand. They're going to California, and, if they can find a
way, to orbit, America will not be held hostage."

Anger blazed behind thick disks of glass. "I'll fight you,
Jeffrey. You'll destroy everything we've worked to build."

"I'd rather destroy it," he said, "than sell it out." And he
turned and walked into the darkened White House.

"They blew up the Lincoln Memorial?" McKay asked in-
credulously. "Well, fuck me to tears."

*"They didn't blow it up exactly. They—it was some kind
of laser. It burned a hole right through the roof. We're still
getting reports."* The voice from Washington was shaking
like a leaf on a branch in a high wind.

Skids was standing in the door of the house, a black mass
against the lantern's wan illumination. Killer had come out
and stood behind Scooter with her chin on his shoulder and
her arms around his chest.

"You guys have no idea how idiotic you look," she said,

"all standing around looking serious and pointing a silver umbrella into the sky."

McKay waved at her to be quiet. "Put a rag in it. They're patching through a message from old Max himself."

"Who?" Scooter asked.

"Chairman Maximov of the FSE," Sloan said quietly, putting one hand to his ear as he did when he was really trying to hear something, even though the speaker was *behind* his ear.

Scooter and Skids looked at each other and wagged their hands with fingers fanned.

"Can we hear?" Scooter asked.

"Yeah," his partner said, "let us hear too."

McKay glared at them. Sloan pulled his communicator from his pocket and thumbed on the external speaker.

". . . *the authority of the Federated States of Europe immediately,*" the deep theatrically accented voice was saying, "*or the might that has been demonstrated to you just now will fall upon you like a veritable fire from heaven. The time has come to cease resistance and surrender to the inevitable—*"

McKay reached over and clicked off Sloan's communicator. "First it was that weenie Geoff van Damm and his stupid hydrogen bomb. Then it was Marcus Aurelius Morrigan and his phony AIDS in a drum. Now it's an evil space laser."

He shook his head in disgust. "More cosmic blackmail. Is this shit *never* gonna end?"

CHAPTER
FIFTEEN ────────────

You could still get your kicks on Route 66. You might be doing it in a horse-drawn wagon made out of a wooden box with automobile tires or one made out of the back half of an old station wagon. You might be pedaling along on a mountain bike with an enormous bulging pack on your back. You might be cruising in a rusty red BMW with a big silver methane tank ballooning where the trunk used to be. You might even be skating.

Or you might be bouncing around in the back of a Ford Apache diesel pickup that must have dated from the Eisenhower administration, trying to get comfortable on the tarps that concealed your gear from prying eyes, squinting around at the dry, wind-carved New Mexican landscape in the awful morning sun and trying not to burn your damn hands on the silver exhaust pipes that ran up either side of the back of the cab.

It might not be called 66 anymore, and 40 didn't always follow the old road faithfully. But what the fuck? Nothing was like it used to be. The end of the world kind of had that effect.

McKay shifted his weight off whatever it was gouging in his left butt cheek and pulled his boonie hat farther over his eyes. *Why would anybody live in this godforsaken part of the world?* he wondered.

Not much of anybody *did*, as far as he could tell. They'd parted company with southbound I-25 on Albuquerque's northern fringe, at the entrance to the newly constructed bypass, in hopes it would live up to its name and let them bypass the greater part of the permanent traffic jam that choked most of America's urban areas and environs. Unfortunately a lot of citizens fleeing Albuquerque's portion of Armageddon had decided to take the ring bypass when the more southerly bridges across the Rio Grande gridlocked, so its bridge had wound up just as blocked.

However, lots of people still did want to get their kicks on 66. As more and more trade had begun to move, the roads were beginning to be opened up again by the people who needed to use them. On the ring bypass bridge, a lane had been cleared by the simple expedient of dumping all the hulks from one lane into the river without even filing an environmental impact statement.

Now Albuquerque and the looming wall of mountains that overlooked the city on the east lay behind them, and they were making their way through what appeared to McKay's jaundiced eyes to be just plain desperate desert. Sam Sloan was driving the Apache, and Tom Rogers was up riding shotgun. Casey was in the bed, sitting and shooting the shit with Skids and Scooter, who rode with their backs to the cab like the old Navajo women in the trucks that passed from time to time, going the other way.

"I just can't believe it," Skids was saying, shaking his head. "I actually had a shot at the bearded guy and blew it. What a tool."

"You hit him, man," Casey said. "That's what you needed to do."

"Yeah. But *you* would have nailed him right through the head. I'm a tool."

Casey grinned. Scooter and Skids had read about the
Guardians in *Parade*. Like everybody else in America.

"You never did say where you know this fucker from,"
McKay observed. He still felt just a twitch of suspicion. Of
course, that was because he was just a nasty, suspicious asshole. And, of course, that was why he was still *alive*.

Skids shrugged. "We've run into him here and there,"
Scooter said guardedly.

"He was with the bunch that took out the Leaping Weasel," Skids said darkly. "He led the sons of bitches to us,
I'm pretty sure."

McKay was about to ask why the hell they called themselves the Leaping Weasel Coop, but a familiar and not well-
loved voice said in his ear, *"Get your thumb out of your butt
and take a look to the south of you, McKay. We got a bit of
genuine Southwestern color coming up."*

They'd left Levy in the care of the Claytonians, or whatever
the hell you called them. Like most people the Guardians had
encountered since the war, they were willing enough to help
out as long as it wouldn't expose them too directly to danger.
The thought that sheltering the wounded flight crewman might
stir up the road gypsies didn't daunt them much; they were
right up against Forrie's goons on a pretty much daily basis,
anyway, and anything that would piss them off was just fine
with the townspeople. Especially after the Guardians made
the clinic a donation of a couple of the gold one-ounce coins
each of them carried in hidden compartments of their coveralls, in direct defiance of Maggie Connoly's orders.

Mayor Husack had been a bit nervous about helping them.
"We can't afford no space-laser attack," he said. "We're just
barely getting by as it is."

Sam Sloan had assured him the space-laser people would
never know they'd helped the Guardians, and helped assuage
his fears by overpaying him ten gold ounces for his old spare
truck.

There had been a certain amount of private debate among
the Guardians when the Leaping Weasel trio invited themselves along for the ride to California. Billy McKay's natural

inclination was to say there were four Guardians, and if God or Major Crenna had thought there ought to be more, one or the other would have set it up that way. His experience in what the Soviets termed "special designation" work—*Spetsnaz* originally referred to *Western* special forces—had been heavily weighted to classic SOG missions on the model of the OPLAN 34 penetrations of North Vietnam during that conflict: paint your face, swim ashore, slit some throats, plant some bombs, and blow out as quiet as the wind. For that you used a small, tight team, no room for indiges or amateurs.

On the other hand, Tom was Special Forces, which meant his training and experience were keyed primarily to cadre work—raising, training, and deploying local assets—though he'd done more than his share of knife-in-the-teeth creepy-crawly commando stuff on loan to Delta and other less well-known public-service organizations. He was perfectly in his element working with indiges, whether they were Vietnamese, Guatemalan Indians, or middle-class Americans.

McKay had let his buddies talk him into letting the three come with them. The Guardians were supposed to be helping America rebuild itself, not doing the job all by themselves. Tom Rogers reckoned it wasn't a bad thing to give American survivors some exposure to the way real experts fought. They weren't totally green, Sloan pointed out, and had done a fair job of helping Rogers save their parts from the road gypsies. And Casey said you could always use a few extra pairs of eyes peeled for MiGs.

It was a variation of that last argument that decided McKay. The Guardians were hard-core heroes but they weren't bulletproof. The New Mexicans could serve as bullet magnets, if nothing else. The Guardians could always lose them like a penetrator round shedding its sabot if they had to.

The Guardians had hit a cache in the mountains northwest of Santa Fe, and aside from completely re-outfitting themselves—the cache was cherry, containing everything but a new armored vehicle to replace the one they'd left in Wyoming—they'd picked up some spare communicators tuned to their channel. Because they didn't want them, or more specifically their scrambler units, falling into the wrong hands, they were cautious about letting their little helpers get their hands on them. At the moment the only one out was attached to the trim hip of their Harley-borne scout.

"What," McKay asked, "you see some drunk Indians sleeping in the road?"

"Don't be racist, McKay," Sloan said primly from the driver's seat.

"Not quite," Killer said.

McKay stirred, looked out over the sun-faded lip of the truck bed. Killer was sitting her Harley on the left shoulder maybe half a klick ahead, pointing. A spur of railroad line was converging with the highway from the south, running through a cut beneath the road. There was something moving along the track, roughly in the same direction they were.

McKay squinted. "What the fuck?" He couldn't make any sense of it *at all*.

"It's a little sail-powered car," Sloan said excitedly. *"Like an old-time handcar with a mast instead of one of those reciprocating lever things. Son of a gun."*

Sure enough, as it got closer, McKay could see it was a little thing about the size of a Honda Accord set on miniature versions of train wheels, taking advantage of the brisk desert wind with a billowing white triangle of sail.

"Wow! Flippy—really flippy," Scooter said. He and Skids waved frantically to the car's lone occupant. He waved back once, very cool himself, and then the sail car passed under the freeway and off to the northwest.

McKay settled himself back down. It was too weird for him. He was used to really scaly shit, decomposing bodies and artillery barrages going off over his head, that kind of thing. But you ran into stuff in the wake of the One-Day War where, as far as he was concerned, the only way to keep your sanity was to try to catch some Z's and pretend you never saw it.

He dozed for a couple of minutes. When he came back to the world, it wasn't any cooler or prettier, and the sun was dead overhead. Casey and the Weasels had gotten themselves worked up over something, which was probably what woke him up.

"You know the Sacker?" Scooter was asking excitedly, and Casey was grinning and nodding his head. "Wow, that's great!"

"Yeah. I met him at . . . what? San Diego Comicon in '89."

"What the fuck's a Sacker?" McKay asked.

"He's a really heavy-duty underground comix artist," Casey said.

"A legend in his own time," said Scooter.

"A legend in his own mind," amended Skids.

"We got a situation developing here, McKay," Killer reported.

He stirred, sitting up to peer around between the Apache's twin stacks. There was no sign of the biker woman, just a shimmering, silver-black asphalt band climbing the next ridge half a klick ahead.

"What? You about to go on the rag and feel PMS coming on?"

"McKay!" Sloan said, outraged.

"Back off, butt head. We got a couple of State Police cruisers nose to nose across the road. I don't think they saw me. I'm gonna cut around cross-country. I'll cover while you go through, in case you fuck up and need a hand."

"Hey, that'll be the fucking day. Anything you grow here in New Mexico, we eat for breakfast."

Killer was still toting the M-249 she'd scarfed at the battle site. They never had turned up any linked 5.56 belts, but the great thing about the SAW was that it would eat standard NATO 5.56 magazines, too, in BAR-emulating mode. Whether a whole boatload of ammo had found its way into circulation before the war despite ever-tightening restrictions on gun ownership, or because the Effsees had imported so much of the stuff, which had then been liberated—or more likely both—it was one thing there never seemed to be a shortage of. McKay was actually not at all unhappy to have her covering them with the MG, which she looked to know how to use, but he'd die before he let on.

"You were at Comicon '89?" Skids asked Casey. "Really?" Casey nodded. "Did you go to that one panel where this goober showed up late and scrambled under the table and almost crawled up Melinda Snodgrass's skirt?"

"What a babe," Scooter remarked dreamily.

"Yeah, I was." Case gazed off over the landscape, which was gashed here and there with steep-sided arroyos. "I always kind of had the hots for her—"

"What?" Skids demanded. "And you didn't go for it? A big, cool Guardian guy like you?"

"Like, I wasn't a Guardian then."

"All right, you clowns," McKay said, "stay awake. We got a State Police roadblock coming up. Keep your pieces out of sight and don't make any moves unless we do."

"We're cool," Skids said, slipping his big T.R. rifle farther under the tarp.

"Yeah, we'll follow your lead." Scooter was trying to lower his voice an octave and not really making it. McKay shook his head and reminded himself that the two had actually seen action and lived.

Casey was checking the magazine on his usual short-range piece, a .45 Ingram with a big Sionics suppressor screwed on the front. In the cab, Sloan and Rogers made their own preparations. McKay said nothing to them; there was no need.

He stashed several grenades in a fold of tarp, just in case Sloan's silver tongue didn't slide them through. It was tough deciding among their usual choices—stun bombs were always a favorite, but if these State Police were like all the other State Police in the world, they'd be wearing shades even if it was the stroke of midnight, and anyway, they'd have to be crazy not to in this sun, and sunglasses cut the dazzle effect. CS was a possibility, but Skids and Scooter didn't have masks and might freak. There was always white phosphorus, of course, if the party got really heavy, but you wanted to make sure you threw one of *those* far enough that none of the flakes got on anything you were serious about keeping, like transport or your body parts. He set down one of each.

Sloan kept them rolling at the seventy-kilometer-per-hour

pace they'd been maintaining since hitting Route 66. There weren't many derelict vehicles forty klicks out of town, but none of them trusted the old truck to go much faster. Chairman Max hadn't even deigned to put a time limit on his ultimatum. He seemed to be taking the position his little orbital toy gave him such an unanswerable advantage, he didn't need to bother; he could always burn out anybody who gave him any back chat. That meant the Guardians weren't racing a deadline to California, not that they were in any position to kick back and pick their bunions, either.

They crested the ridge. The State Police roadblock was about six hundred meters ahead. There was a third vehicle parked by the side of the road.

"Look casual," McKay said.

A cop with a huge gut stuffed into a black uniform with gray stripes down the leg stood in front of the cars parked nose to nose, waving for them to stop. Half a dozen officers covered from behind the cruisers with M16s and riot guns. Several more stood by the side of the road, talking to somebody in the third car.

"How can they stand to wear black in this heat?" Sloan asked.

He braked, stopped about ten nonthreatening meters short of the barricade. The officer who'd waved them down swaggered forward with sunlight dancing intolerably bright on the black leather bill of his cap. Two more tentatively came forward behind him. The one on Tom's side had a Thompson submachine gun, of all things.

"Who are you and where you going?" the cop demanded in a Latino accent, rapping the backs of his knuckles on the driver's door.

"We're just down outa the Espanola Valley," Sloan said in his thickest Ozark hick voice, trying hard not to notice the cop was waving his hand in the air to cool knuckles sizzled on the sun-hot metal. "We're headin' into Arizona an' look for work. Ain't no law against that, is there?"

"You got papers?"

"We maybe got a few copies of the Albuquerque *Journal*

in the back to wipe our butts on. Whadda you think, son? Are the Effsees still here, expect us to have passports just to cross the damn state line—"

"Holy shit, Chavo," the man with the tommy gun yelped, "I know these dudes! It's them—it's the Guardians!"

CHAPTER
SIXTEEN ————————————

Tom raised his right hand, which he'd been holding out of sight between his legs. It held a .45 with a long fat silencer screwed on the end. He fired through the windshield and hit the Thompson man smack between the eyes.

Sam Sloan yanked up the handle of the door and slammed it open. Its metal rim caught the Latino cop in the face, knocking off his cap and sending him reeling back. Sloan put a foot down onto the blistering blacktop, raised his MP5, and fired a three-round burst into the man with the M16 who'd been backing the fat cop on his side.

Making a lightning decision, McKay whipped the stun grenade forward over the Apache's cab. It landed a couple meters shy of the roadblock and started going off with a series of flashes and deafening bangs. As he hoped, the troopers behind the blocking cars ducked in sheer confusion.

He was already coming up with the surprise he'd had tucked away beneath the tarp: a Maremont M-60E3 7.62-mm machine gun. It was cut down a bit from the full-dress M-60 but didn't lack a foot-pound of its ferocious firepower. Holding it by front and rear pistol grips, he dropped it onto the roof of the Apache and fired a long burst right where the cars met. White steam exploded from under hoods buckled by repeated impact as the radiators ruptured.

Casey had flung himself to the right side of the truck bed and was hosing the car parked by the road with wild bursts that sent the men beside it diving into the ditch. The person they'd been talking to improvidently popped up out of the vehicle on the far side, his curiosity to see what was going down apparently causing sudden brain lock.

"It's him!" Skids Rodey shrieked. *"It's the bearded guy!"* The truck rocked on its suspension as he leapt to his feet and began levering off rounds from the hip like Chuck Connors as *The* fucking *Rifleman.*

In a handy interval between pumping bursts into the cop mobiles—you didn't want to just hold the trigger back, even with a real MG—McKay risked a glance sideways. Damned if he didn't see the same face he'd seen gloating over the sights of a .44 Magnum yesterday, looking right at him. The road gypsy had on what seemed to be the same leather jacket over bandages that enshrouded the left side of his body. A bullet from Skids's .30-06 sprayed him with glass from a wing mirror and he dived out of sight.

As McKay gaped at the mysterious apparition of the bearded guy, his temporary fire superiority began to slip. A brave soul popped up from behind the right-hand cruiser, blasting away over the trunk with an autoloading Benelli shotgun. McKay heard Sloan yelp as a well-aimed or lucky blast blew what remained of the windshield in over him. McKay twitched the barrel right and pulled the trigger. A sort of red mist seemed to shimmer briefly behind the shotgunner, and he blew away like a tumbleweed in a desert wind.

"You okay, Sam?"

"Fine, except I've got a lapful of powdered glass."

Scooter had scrambled over the tailgate and was kneeling behind the truck. The fat cop whose face Sloan had rammed the door into was starting to recover, pulling out a revolver even bigger and shinier than Sloan's nickel-plated Python. Scooter blasted him, then turned his fire on the blocking cars.

"C'mon and eat it, creeps!" he shouted. "Eat it, eat it, *eat it*!"

The car bodies undoubtedly blocked most of his 7.62-mm slugs. As the cops sheltering behind found out, the vehicles shielded them not at all from McKay's full-size rounds. One of them burst from behind the northerly car, diving and rolling behind a clump of some kind of broomstick-dry crud that passed for vegetation in this part of the world, then the two took off running up the road.

McKay let them run. These were not the hard-core types who were going to track them down and slit their throats for vengeance, after all, and the car on the south half of the highway was already burning. When the car radios were taken out, the survivors would have no chance to report their presence, anyway. There was no point wasting the bullets.

He let the Maremont rest on the cab, reached to his belt, said, "Willy Peter" for the benefit of his buddies, and neatly tossed the grenade through the window of the car on the shoulder.

Casey and, presumably, the other two Guardians obediently ducked. Skids stood howling like an idiot and cranking off rounds from a revolver, his Winchester having run dry. McKay grabbed him by the suspenders and yanked him down on his ass on the tarp-covered mound of gear.

"What the heck?" Skids asked.

Whoom, the grenade said.

A beat later the bombed cruiser's gas tank whooshed off, sending a big orange ball of flame skyward and singeing the eyebrows of Billy McKay, who like a choad-headed boot had decided to peer over the truck bed to admire his handiwork. It got awful hot all of a sudden.

"Ouch, fuck. Move us along, Sloan. Or is this beast broken?"

In reply, the truck bucked and rolled forward. "We're fine, Billy. But I'd like to get this stuff brushed off my crotch."

"Do it later. You ain't gettin' head anytime in the near future. The bad guys are gonna wanna know where all this smoke is coming from, even if our little friends didn't get much chance to get any radio calls off."

Skids was helping haul Scooter over the tailgate. As they bounced into the shallow median depression—flushing a terrified state cop, who dashed all the way across the eastbound lanes and out into the desert without anybody paying attention—the northernmost of the cars parked across the road blew up too. McKay put a burst into the rear end of the other one. It joined the others in flames.

"I can't believe it," Skids said, sitting with his back to the cab, feeding fresh cartridges into his rifle. "The bearded guy—son of a bitch!"

"What the hell was he doing with the State Police? He sure didn't look like no prisoner to me."

Scooter shrugged. "State Police were pretty thick with the Effsees, for the most part. And they've never seemed exactly hostile to the road gypsies, if you know what I mean."

"But why would the State Police jump us?" Sloan asked.

"You boys sure acted like you expected them to jump your action," Killer said. She was still away out of sight. *"Why the big surprise?"*

"We're paranoid. That's why we're still around. Somebody puts a bomb in your goddam airplane, it sours your outlook on people, you know?"

"How's Scooter?"

"A little nutso, but okay." McKay looked at the individual in question. " 'Eat it, eat it, eat it'?"

Scooter shrugged.

"Isn't he sweet?" Killer's voice asked.

Clear of the flaming wreckage, Sloan brought them back onto the road and up to speed. McKay popped open the receiver of his M-60 and dropped the plastic half-moon ammo box. It held half a belt of 7.62 linked, and he'd burned up most of it. He rooted through the other booty from the cache—rations, ammo, a couple of ARMBRUST antitank rocket launchers for good measure—until he found another half-moon box. They came from Australia, and they were great for keeping the cranky ammunition belts from tangling; they made it possible to do completely without an assistant gunner, which in a four-man team was a definite plus.

"Shouldn't we, like, leave the highway?" Casey wondered.

"Naw," McKay said. "If the Staties come out in any force, they'll be making a beeline for the big smoke. We run into a random patrol, they ain't likely to bug us—we're just another truckful of hayseeds."

"That bunch sure tried to bug us," Sloan said.

"Yeah. And we kicked their butts and took their names. Any other loose Staties we meet up with are gonna be a piece of cake too." He slammed shut the feed-tray lid.

"Think about something real," McKay went on. "Somebody in Washington spiked us with a bomb. Forrie's biker boys seemed to be waiting for whatever was left of us to hit the ground. Now the New Mexico State Police turns up in the company of a road gypsy who was trying to croak us yesterday. Do we detect a pattern here?"

"Washington hasn't, like, seemed too secure lately," remarked Casey Wilson, who'd pulled his rifle out from under the tarp and was skinning it out of its ripstop case. It was sort of a security thing with him. "And people've been trying to assassinate us a lot lately."

"Come now," Sloan said. *"Isn't that a little paranoid?"*

"No," McKay and Casey said in unison.

"Well, I grant there have been some instances, like the bomb in that briefing chamber in Chicago . . . but still, Washington says the Romans are still active. I'd think they'd be inclined to be a little vengeful."

"But there's only so far you can ride this Roman hobbyhorse," McKay said. "I mean, if they're so pissed off and so powerful, why don't they step in and take over?"

"Isn't it great listening in on one side of a conversation?" Skids asked Scooter.

"But they're not *that powerful. That's why they have to resort to assassination."*

"Trying to assassinate us halfway across the continent isn't powerful? Shit, President Jeff can't hardly get people to do what he wants as far away as Georgetown, except for us."

Casey frowned. "Billy, do you hear something?"

"No. Just this wind blowing on our heads. Christ, it's getting hot out here."

A low mesa with a palisade of red sandstone running around the top of it paralleled the road to the south here. McKay happened to be gazing idly that way when a helicopter popped up from behind it. Just like that.

"Holy *shit*!" he yelled. For a moment the beast just hovered there, seeming to peer at them with blank malevolence, the silenced engines and specially constructed rotors all but silent.

"Apache," Casey remarked with a certain amount of interest. A helicopter was an aircraft, after all.

"What is it?" Scooter and Skids were asking, more or less in unison.

"We're fucked, is what," McKay answered, making himself abruptly very busy. He had recognized the weird, drooped dachshund nose just as Casey spoke. "Sam, do something."

"You got it, McKay," Sam said. He didn't have a lot of ideas *what* he was going to do. He hoped his left brain was going to come through in the crunch.

The attack helicopter swept forward like some great hunting bird. Sloan pressed the accelerator down, making the ancient diesel fart in dismay, driving with one eye on the road and one on the helicopter. He was hoping to find a nice abandoned semi to hide behind. Of course, there's never one around when you need it.

His intuition was in that day. He whipped the wheel hard left just as an orange light began to flash beneath the chopper's nose. The land-borne Apache went broadside and heeled way, way over in a screeching of tires as the 30-mm burst fired by its aerial namesake chain-sawed the blacktop not ten meters ahead.

Scooter blazed away at the olive-green shadow as it flashed by overhead. Skids stared after it, rifle in hand, dubious of his ability to track the lean, vicious craft with his scope.

"Why didn't you shoot at it, McKay?"

" 'Cause my 60'd do the same to it as Scooter's AK, which is dick. Those pukes are *armored*."

The chopper pitched up and went into a turn, tauntingly

slow. Sloan sent the truck bucketing across the median, across the eastbound lanes—swerving to dodge a dead Subaru that was way too small to shelter behind—and right off the road. Three strands of barbed wire parted in a weird metallic chord as the occupants went bouncing around the truckbed, cursing and hollering.

"What's he doing?" Skids wondered aloud. "Casey, could you, like, get your foot out of my ear?"

"Sorry, man."

What Sloan had been doing had been ditching into an arroyo that cut beneath the highway. The culvert wasn't big enough to pass the truck but they could scramble into it if all else failed. In any event, the dry streambed did serve to get them out of the chopper's immediate field of fire, and it was the only thing approaching cover they had any chance of reaching in time to do any good.

McKay had kept hold of the object he was working on. It was going to be their only chance to avoid, at best, a long walk in the hot sun—and the arroyo was probably not so deep that the Apache couldn't virtually land in it and sweep them out with its chain gun if they took shelter inside it. . . .

Still, it was there. "Bail out, everybody," he ordered. "Into the culvert."

"But—" Sloan began.

"You done your part. Now *boogie*."

The AH-64 was taking its sweet time swinging back around. It was probably calling in its contact report and just kind of fucking with their minds. *If they were in any doubt we were us,* McKay thought, *Scooter firing 'em up probably took care of that.* To be fair, this was almost certainly not the only pickup on this stretch of highway this afternoon to have at least one automatic weapon riding shotgun, and anyway, the chopper had opened fire first. But McKay wasn't in the mood to be fair.

Sloan was tail-end Charlie diving into the culvert. The helicopter swept overhead, so low that its tires must have come close to brushing the guardrail on the highway.

McKay shouldered the ARMBRUST launcher. Most of the things you could hit on an Apache attack chopper were ar-

mored to take hits from anything up to a 25 mike-mike. At
least that's what the specs said, and while McKay was as
skeptical as anybody else with half a brain about the discrepancy
between what it said in the specs and what you got in
the field, this was not the time or place to put those claims
to the test. The ARMBRUST would bust the armor carapace
of a main battle tank. It would make short work of any protection
the chopper could lift.

If he could only *hit* the motherfucker.

He'd been hoping the thing would just hover to fire them
up. Apparently its pilot wasn't all that eager to see how bulletproof
the Lexan windscreen really was, either. It whispered
two hundred meters down the arroyo and went into a
tight-banking turn.

The monster was just going to take as many passes at them
as it took. This was going to be McKay's best shot. He sighted
down the fat plastic tube and fired.

The ARMBRUST was flashless, recoilless, and not real
loud. As the missile streaked toward the target McKay saw
the shimmering of sunlight on a circle of steel and realized
that the fucking rotor disk was between the rocket and the
ship itself.

There was a chance the rocket would miss the rotor—but
it didn't. There was an eye-searing white flash and a crack
like God's own shinbone snapping. McKay tasted hot puke
in his throat. A foot of open space was enough to dissipate
the force of a shaped-charge armor-busting warhead like the
one the ARMBRUST carried. The chopper's armor could take
it, easy.

He forgot that the *rotor* couldn't. One blade sheared right
next to the hub. The chopper rolled onto its back and slammed
into the side of a low purplish hill.

McKay was sitting back on the tarp-covered pile of gear
when his comrades emerged from the culvert. He was lighting
up a cigar—a gift from the well-pleased Mayor Husack—
and admiring the helicopter's funeral pyre.

"See?" he said. "I told you. Piece of cake."

• • •

The airplane was a Cessna, a barbed white arrowhead with the prop in the rear, a canard bone in the nose, and a gun tray slung beneath.

"Smuggler buster," Casey remarked with a certain amount of distaste. "Old DEA job." He was not overly impressed with an aircraft whose main mission was shooting down Piper Cubs and shooting up RVs suspected of running dope.

Skids and Scooter exchanged doubtful looks. "Aren't we, uh, kind of exposed out here?"

McKay took a deep drag on his cigar. "Naw. They don't even know we exist. *Watch.*"

Sure enough, the Cessna hunter-killer cruised on at speed to the east without so much as banking for a better look at them. It was looking for a truck, after all, a very specific truck.

Not some unlikely-looking conveyance rolling down the railroad under a triangular sail, with six passengers perched atop a mound of baggage like so many baby oppossums.

It had taken a healthy portion of their stock of gold ounces—replenished at the cache in the Sangre de Cristos—and, of course, their truck thrown in—with instructions to keep it hidden until sunset—to convince the sail car's owner to part with it. He was a Japanese national, of all things, who had built it himself, and he was very sentimentally attached to it. On the other hand, he was headed for California, anyway, and since he had a map of the railroads, he could almost certainly track the curious vehicle to wherever they left it when they were done with it.

It was slow, and dependent on the vagaries of the wind. But it was going their way and was the last thing on earth their pursuers would expect to find them on or in. And anyway, wind didn't seem to be in too short supply out here.

Killer called in to say the airplane had continued patrolling toward Albuquerque until it was out of sight. McKay went to sleep.

When a gingerly hand on McKay's arm brought him awake, all that remained of day was an orange band along the horizon, being squeezed out of sight beneath a lowering cap of heavy purple-black. The temperature had dropped sharply, just the way he remembered from the deserts of the Middle East.

The first thing he saw was that the sail was furled. "What the fuck? We're still moving."

"This thing has an engine," Sam Sloan said. "Just a small one, but enough to keep us moving at a reasonable clip." He shook his head. "Here I thought the guy was a purist, and it turns out he's dropped in a mill. Some people."

McKay had no idea what he was talking about, and refused to ask. "Why'd you wake me?"

"It's all over the radio, McKay," Skids said.

"*What's* all over the radio?"

"Maggie Connoly, man," Casey said. "She's, like, telling the whole country it's their duty to go along with Chairman Max. And to do everything they can to resist *us*."

CHAPTER
SEVENTEEN ─────────────────

"I don't believe I will be able to help you, gentlemen," the general said.

Billy McKay blinked at him across the desk. It had been a long way to come to get turned down flat. *Maybe I oughta just kill him.*

He set the clear coffee cup down on the desk with exaggerated care. He could feel the eyes of Sam Sloan and Tom Rogers on him. The four of them were seated on leather-covered chairs in the eternal twilight of Major General Nathan Ebersole's office, surrounded by dark oak paneling and photographs of milestones and celebrities.

None of the pictures had Ebersole in them. A lot of them featured the lean figure and sharply chiseled features of General Marcus Antonius Meadows, the charismatic Vietnam War hero who headed SPACECOM and Vandenberg before the war. When the balloon went up, General Meadows had been in SPACECOM's hardened command center. A one-megaton warhead had landed more or less dead on top of it. After the manner of ground bursts everywhere, it caused extremely lo-

calized heavy damage and extremely indiscriminate fallout,
neither of which did much damage to the physical plant outside the radius of the crater it left. Obviously the Soviets
intended simply to paralyze SPACECOM for the duration of
the war, leaving as much of the Vandenberg launch site as
possible for the victorious Soviet forces—presumably including Nicaraguan and Cuban troops, if the Soviet planners happened to've seen *Red Dawn*—to seize.

Or maybe they just fucked up.

However it had shaken out, what it had shaken out had
been Nate Ebersole, a man of ravaged handsomeness with
gray hair and deep lines eroded down either side of his mouth
who resembled a stooped Sterling Hayden. He'd been a hot
pilot and a fire-eater in his own right who'd gotten his wings
just a bit too late for the Vietnam War and never quite got
over it. No fighter jock ever hungered after combat as avidly
as Nathan Ebersole. But it was a hunger that was never ap-
peased.

McKay knew some of his background. He was as shocked
by the fact that it was No Guts–No Glory Ebersole who was
refusing him as by the refusal itself. He was almost as shocked
to recall that this old man wasn't yet fifty.

Not surprisingly it was Sam Sloan who located his voice
first. Sloan was always the diplomat in the group, though Tom
had the cadreman's knack of getting along with anybody he
cared to.

"Why can't you help us, General?" he asked.

Ebersole looked down at the hands he had folded on the
desktop before him. They were surprisingly large hands, and
surprisingly hard, as if they belonged to a day laborer from
Sonora. It was as if all that had been the dynamic young
general had wasted away except those hands.

"I have blood enough on my hands, gentlemen. I cannot
in conscience take action that will jeopardize further lives.
Innocent lives."

"You don't think it jeopardizes innocent lives if we give in
to blackmail?" It took all of McKay's self-control to keep the
outburst down to a low roar. The general looked at him with
naked appeal in his blue eyes.

"Chairman Maximov is not a good man, nor a just man. I've met him, you know, when I was with NATO in Europe."

It had been typical of his luck that he was awarded what appeared to be the plum position of second in command to Meadows, who defined the Air Force's fast track. But what the appointment really meant was that Ebersole had missed his chance to be theater air commander for the week of conventional warfare preceding the One-Day War.

"But what he is not is a madman. He seeks power, plain and simple. If he obtains it, he will be satisfied." He spread his hands. "And perhaps it would not be such a terrible thing, to have the world unified under one command. Maximov is shrewd and able; the world could have worse rulers, I think."

McKay picked up his cup, because his mouth felt dry and his tongue seemed to have swollen and turned to felt. He glanced down at the black surface and his stomach turned over. *What the hell can you expect from a man with clear coffee cups?*

He had had enough. "Of all the God damned weak-kneed ridiculous pieces of—"

The office door popped open. A round head poked in, with a round nose in the center of it supporting round glasses and a little brown toothbrush mustache above a sphincter of a mouth.

"Euu," the head said, in a peculiarly constipated way. "General, are these men bothering you?"

The general waved a conciliatory hand. "It's okay, Chris. Really. Everything under control."

McKay glared at the interloper. "What the hell is it to you?"

"I could make you leave. I *could*."

"You and what army, pencil-neck?"

"Billy," Tom said.

"Chris, I'm fine. Really. We're just having a disagreement. Now, please, you must excuse us."

The head gave McKay a final myopic glare and left, pulling the door in after it like a turtle's paldron.

"Major Boyd," the general explained. "My chief of security. Really a fine young man, if a trifle overprotective of me.''

"The president, who is your commander in chief as well as ours, has ordered all members of the American armed forces to cooperate with us to the fullest in this emergency.'' Sloan was laying a bit of ice into it now, a bit of his best Steel Commander. He could be enough of a hard-ass to impress even McKay, if he put his back into it. He hadn't gotten to that stage . . . yet.

Ebersole shook his head. "It's not so simple as that. What is the scope of President MacGregor's powers in the present circumstances? Doubts have been raised as to the legitimacy of his succession, and what are his plans for the future? Does he regard himself as dictator? This should be an election year—is he making plans to hold elections? I certainly see none."

"There's a fucking *war* on, General," McKay said. He couldn't hold it inside anymore. Sloan could just kick his ass for him later if he wanted to.

"In the past that's been no excuse for violation of constitutionally mandated procedures. And besides, the war is over. And we, as responsible military men, are bound to follow the dictates of our own consciences should the president act in such a way as to threaten thousands of innocent lives. Have we forgotten the lesson of Nuremberg, gentlemen?''

McKay stood up. His leather chair fell onto its back with a thump. "I can't believe I'm hearing this," he said, and stomped out the door.

"I can't believe it," Billy McKay said. "I can't believe he *said* that shit.''

The sun turned the aprons and runways to burning silver from which the heat shimmer beat like the rhythm of a drum. The young captain who was walking the Guardians to their vehicle—no longer the sail car but a real live Jeep Cherokee— bit his lower lip in consternation.

"The general is a great man," he said. "You have to understand that.''

"He sure as hell doesn't show it," McKay said.

"McKay," Sloan subvocalized warningly over the communicators.

But Captain Filson didn't take offense. He was a wiry, handsome black man who looked about twenty-two, though he had to be older. He regarded the Guardians with overt hero worship and seemed to want to reconcile them with Ebersole at all costs.

"He kept us together after we lost General Meadows in the war. He helped us reclaim the base from the fallout, helped us tend to the injured and those with radiation sickness. He pulled us through the Effsee occupation. He's a man who always does what he sees to be the right thing. *Always.*"

"Well, his vision's sure fucked up right about now," McKay said, savagely biting the end of a cigar.

Filson looked pained. "He lost his daughter in the war, Lieutenant. She was all he had; his wife died of cancer five years ago. Barb was just twenty. She was in flight school herself." He shook his head. "That changed him. I can't deny that. But he's still a good man."

"Yeah," McKay grunted skeptically. "Say, what's the story with this Major Boyd, anyway?"

"You met the Boy? He—" Filson shut up and shook his head.

"He what?" McKay demanded.

"Nothing. But watch out for him. Word to the wise, okay?"

Casey stopped abruptly and grabbed McKay's sleeve. "Billy, look! Wow, oh, wow—look at that, *look.*"

"Yeah, Christ, what's the matter with you, Casey? You act like I'm your mommy and you want me to buy it for you."

He knew perfectly well what was the matter with Casey. It was the needle-slim little F-16 fighter just touching down with a prim squeal of tires on tarmac that was getting him worked up. He *did* want his mommy to buy it for him—or McKay, or anybody. Though he was as dedicated a Guardian as even Billy McKay could ask, he'd never made any pretense that being one was any better than distant second to being a fighter jock. And the Fighting Falcon was *his*, the instrument he played better than any man alive.

Filson beamed and bobbed his head in pride. "We've got

three of them in service. We keep them on-line, armed with a full air-superiority load and ready to go twenty-four hours a day. The general insists on it."

He gave McKay a meaningful sideways glance. McKay felt like holding up cards that said 9.5.

"Only people who can boast more in this part of the world are Edwards AFB, and what they've got is ground-attack planes and some old Phantoms."

"Oh, wow," Casey said.

The wind brought the salt smell of the nearby Pacific to their nostrils. The sky was white with a thin wash of cloud. A flight of shore birds flowed past. McKay stood and stared out across the flats toward a set of launch towers, gray with distance, that had survived the thermonuclear bombardment.

"We've also got an operations-ready orbiter," Filson said, almost in a whisper. "And the boosters, and the tank, and the fuel. We can be ready to go in twenty-four hours, because of the general."

"And you won't go," McKay said, "because of the general."

"I don't like the idea of giving in to Chairman Maximov any better than you do, Lieutenant," Filson said, staring off at the towers. "But the personnel of this base will not go against the general's wishes. Believe it."

"I do," McKay said. "C'mon, let's get out of here. If you're a good little boy, Case, I may get you a Revell model of one of those fuckers, okay?"

"He's a traitor," Billy McKay said firmly.

It was cool and dark in the living room of the house near San Luis Obispo where Morgenstern had his headquarters of the moment, but afternoon sunlight glowed in the atrium beyond with that special golden California glow. The other Guardians were occupying the massive, comfortable furniture while their fearless leader paced and bellowed.

"You are speaking loosely," said the suntanned old man in the black-and-brown-striped robe who stood near the door to the atrium.

McKay threw his glass down. It was a heavy tumbler, and bounded on the blood-red tile floor without breaking.

"*Bull*shit. He's refusing a direct order from the president of the United States. And he was big boss at Vandenberg when the Effsees took the place over, and they didn't remove him. That means he was spreading for 'em, Doc."

"If you would ever learn to think in a systematic way, Lieutenant," Dr. Jacob Morgenstern said, unperturbed, "you could be quite dangerous. Fortunately you've not yet shown any propensity for developing the knack of Western linear thought."

McKay turned on the man, breathing heavily, eyebrows lowered and nostrils flared. There was only one man on Earth who could talk to him that way. Unfortunately this was him.

"He was a collaborator. Do we have to let him get away with that?"

"A lot of people collaborated during the Effsee incursion, McKay," Sloan said, treading as softly as he could.

"Well, we ought to do something about them too. We need to clear the goddam traitors out. Everybody who helped the fucking Effsees in the least little way."

"Marla Eklund and her people were helping the Effsees when we first ran into them, Billy," Tom said.

McKay stopped pacing and worked his jaw for a while. In point of fact, Marla Eklund and her platoon had *arrested* them. And Marla was the closest thing McKay had these days to a regular squeeze, unless she was so pissed off that she'd never speak to him again after she'd caught him porking the daughter of the president of the Republic of Texas.

"Not everyone enjoys your robust clarity of vision, Lieutenant McKay," Morgenstern said. "To a good many people, not all of whom were evil or cowardly or even foolish, the rights and wrongs of that situation were not easy to discern. The Federated States of Europe Expedition Force brought with them, you will no doubt recall, the last elected president of the United States. In spite of the fact that he had vanished in the missle attack and the chief justice pronounced him legally dead, Jeffrey MacGregor's succession could not help but smack of usurpation.

"Besides"—he sipped wine, red, not white—"open defiance of the FSE occupiers wasn't a luxury everyone could afford. General Ebersole's command consisted of a handful of personnel trying to survive the aftermath of a hydrogen bomb. There were still large pockets of lethal emitters around Vandenberg when the Effsees arrived. Staunch resistance might have been what Rambo would do, but it's not apparent that it would have been either the practical or moral course."

McKay was breathing heavily, as if he'd just run five miles. "Okay. But he's still refusing to obey orders from his commander in chief. And there's this whole Connoly thing—I got half a mind to go back to Washington and straighten that bitch out."

He knew as soon as he'd said it that he'd fucked up. He *knew* it.

"Half a mind, Lieutenant, is precisely what—no, I can't say it, you leave yourself too vulnerable. The idiom 'taking candy from a baby' suggests itself." *Sip.* "Suffice it to say that you have your own orders from the president, and nothing has happened to alter or invalidate them."

"Dr. Connoly's got a right to her opinions, Billy," Rogers said.

McKay stared at his buddy as if the soft-spoken ex–Green Beret had admitted to being a KGB mole. "What kind of shit is that? She's going directly against the president. On the fucking *radio*. On *Forrie Smith's* channel. Jesus!"

"What Dr. Connoly is doing is disloyal in the personal sense," Sloan said, "but it's not treasonous. The right to free speech is still in effect, last I heard—and if it's not, I quit, because the Constitution is what we're pledged to defend, first and foremost."

It occurred to McKay to say, *all right, go ahead and quit, you pussy.* But a red light was blinking on and off inside his head, the well-worn Billy McKay Asshole Indicator. He inhaled deeply and let it all out in an explosive gust.

"All right. But just like you say, Doc, we got our orders, and we ain't carrying them out just sitting here on our hands. Maybe Vandenberg's overdue for a change of command. If that wuss Ebersole won't help us, we're gonna have to take matters into our own hands.''

"With what, Billy?" Tom asked. "Ebersole seems real popular with his people. If we take him out, *we* won't be. What will we do then? Try to make 'em launch us into orbit at gunpoint?"

McKay glared at him. "All right," he said. "Bad idea."

He turned to Morgenstern. "But in the morning we're gonna go out and have a nice little talk with Ebersole, see if we can get him to see the light. This ain't over yet."

Morgenstern looked dubious but said nothing.

"And if you don't want us to lean hard on your dear, sweet, misunderstood general, Doctor, maybe you better kind of shake it up and find this magical, mystical Blueprint launch facility that's supposed to be out here.''

Morgenstern was not a man who took any shit from *anybody*. But when a body had a point, he could take what he dished out. He nodded briskly.

"I'm doing what I can, McKay. My network is making inquiries, but there's nothing concrete to report."

"All right," McKay said.

"And I'll talk to the general myself. I know the man. His daughter's death broke his spirit, but he still has a streak of his old stubbornness. I may be able to reason with him. If not''—he smiled thinly through his trim, grizzled beard— "perhaps the prospect of a return visit will frighten him enough to bring him around."

"I fuckin' hope so. And tell that little weenie Major Boyd to stay out of our way.''

"I shall."

The other Guardians rose and started out. "McKay?" Morgenstern said.

McKay stopped and looked around.

"Before you go, pick up that glass you threw down."

CHAPTER
EIGHTEEN

They were driving down one of the feeder roads that led off California 246, across the Santa Ynez River, and on to Vandenberg, when the blacktop began to bubble like boiling tar twenty meters ahead of the black Cherokee with which Morgenstern's network had supplied them the day before.

Casey let out a yelp, hit the brake, and swerved frantically left. Sam, beside him, and Rogers in the rear seat were belted in and all right. McKay, however, was riding as he preferred to in carryall vehicles like this, in back on some tarps where he could sprawl his long legs out. He went tumbling all around the rear like a pinball on a real bonus roll before fetching up against the rear of the front seat.

"Jesus *Christ*, Casey, what the fuck are you doing?" he bellowed. "Hey, what's that smell, hot metal?"

He let the sentence go, staring blankly at the little chunk of sky where the top left corner of the Cherokee's rear used to be.

Casey's maneuver had been so wild that the Jeep skidded broadside and slewed around a hundred and eighty degrees, facing straight back along the road they'd taken by the time the right-hand wheels raised a spume of white dust and crushed seashells where the pavement ran out.

There was a strange rushing, roaring sound, like a jet on full throttle, and he was pretty sure it wasn't just the blood pounding in his ears.

He cranked the wheel left again, gunned it, dragging his starboard tires out of the dust. He caught a glimpse of a shimmer of heat ahead of him, and then the asphalt was bubbling in a diagonal slash across the road.

He already had the vehicle in motion, screaming around in as tight a turn as he could hold. The wheelbase was too long for him to pull as small a radius as he liked, but his right wheels only spewed up a quick spray of dust before he was firmly on the pavement and lining out once more for the two-kilometer-distant gates of Vandenberg.

He didn't have a hope in hell of reaching them; they didn't even enter the lightning calculations in his fighter pilot's brain. What he needed was overhead cover, and *fast*.

It was the orbital laser—he'd known that from the first weird eruption of the pavement almost under his front tires. From the diagrams they'd been shown, Cygnus X-1's gross aiming was done by compressed-gas attitude jets, but fine adjustments were carried out by a series of mirrors. They were capable of incredible precision and excellent real-time control.

But the laser had been designed primarily to take out huge targets that, while moving very fast, followed a path as easily predictable as the moon's. Not a little scurrying bug on Earth's surface that could dodge randomly in two dimensions . . .

Or even three, if the bug's controlling brain was cunning enough.

Casey cut right, into the scrub. The invisible sword cut a steaming line right down the lane they'd occupied a moment before. One of his New Age surfer beach buddies of a lifetime before would've credited the timing of his dodge to some kind of psychic power. When it came to combat, Casey Wilson was a stone rationalist: he knew intuition prompted him, but there was nothing mystical about it. It was a combat pilot's instinct for targeting solutions and how to spoil them, for knowing which move the other fellow was going to make.

It was just another dogfight. It didn't matter that he had the bad guy neatly trapped in his six-o'clock position as no fighter jock in history ever had, nor that he couldn't dive or climb. This was *his* game, and he was the best living player of it.

He veered and darted crazily across white landscape dotted with clumps of green, braking and accelerating unpredictably, spinning wheels and skidding but never losing control. His buddies clung on with white knuckles and whiter faces. They knew their lives were completely in his hands.

"Get ready to bail out," he said conversationally.

The unseen beam swept across the hood of the Cherokee in a coruscating shower of sparks. Steam erupted from the radiator, obscuring Casey's vision as the vehicle plunged down a short bank and splashed into the Santa Ynez River.

Guardians burst out of the Jeep in all directions. McKay couldn't get the rear gate to open with two quick jerks. The second bent the handle, so he butt-stroked the window out with his Maremont and dived through. His initial thought had been fear that he'd get trapped inside a sinking vehicle and drown, but he realized how unfounded that fear was as he plowed bottom sand with his chin.

He came up sputtering and splashing. Casey had brought the Cherokee down right beside the wooden road bridge. It didn't clear the shallow water by enough to permit the vehicle to get under it, but there was plenty of room for the four Guardians to scramble to at least momentary safety.

"Good job, Case," McKay grunted, getting a good combat grip on his machine gun, which was not going to do a whole hell of a lot of good but did make him feel better. Casey acknowledged the compliment with a shy grin. He had already snapped back from Chuck Yeager to slightly shy California kid. That probably showed he was schiz, but what the hell?

"Is this bridge thick enough to keep off the laser?" Sloan asked, dubiously eying the creosoted timbers close overhead.

"Who knows, man?" Casey said. "Probably not for very long."

The laser slashed down the river toward them in a billowing, roaring cloud of steam. The Jeep exploded in a yellow fireball as the invisible beam of light took it.

Andreas Krieger cursed. "They've gotten under a bridge!"

Whistling "Londonderry Air" under his breath, Dr. John Mallory frowned distractedly at the screen on his own console, which was repeating the high-res satellite image most of the others were watching on the control room's big color LCD screen. For all the miracles the folded optics and computer filtering and enhancement systems on board the surveillance satellite—circling in a different orbit and height from their own—could perform, on his small screen, at least, it was hard to make much sense of what was going on.

He checked the displays flickering on his board. "Can we burn through?" Sanjitay asked.

"Take too much time," rust-haired Macchio murmured.

"Doctor," Sylvie Braestrop said, her voice as clear and resonant as a bell, "our window for the main target will close in one hundred seconds."

Mallory glanced up at Hocevar, hanging like a watchful demon in the center of the control room. The black-clad Hungarian nodded once.

Damn him for his presumption in reading my mind and giving me leave to do what I intended!

"Let them go," he said. "They're just four men. And once we hit our main objective, there'll be little they or any man can do to touch us."

The F-16 dropped form the clear California morning sky as lightly as a snowflake—or, less inappropriately to the climate, a fleck of paint chipped off the sky's blue ceiling, which its blue-gray, low-visibility color scheme made it resemble. Its wheels swung from its trim belly, reaching coyly out to greet the tarmac.

And then the aircraft vanished in a bloom of yellow and orange. Flaming debris splashed down the runway.

The laser swept on, exploding a second Fighting Falcon on its apron. The aircraft were merely targets of opportunity, not the true objective.

Though the watchers on the ground, staring in stunned amazement, could not tell it, the laser winked off as servo-motors made minute adjustments to the aiming mirrors. Then the beam winked back on, unseen as before.

But if the beam itself could not be seen, its effects were only too visible. The thin-gauge metal of the roof of the giant gleaming box that was the surviving Vehicle Assembly Building—spared by a freak of blast dynamics from the force of the warhead that had struck nearby—puffed away in vapor as the beam stabbed through.

From the Expeditionary Force's reports—confirmed by a much more recent communication—the occupants of Cygnus knew where their main target rested, even though they could not see it directly. The beam worked in a brief box pattern, then cut crisscross through the middle of it. When it went out again, the Vandenberg shuttle lay in several pieces.

The quiescent laser's focus moved on again. It overlooked several huge subterranean tanks of fuel and liquid oxygen. They were buried deeply and cushioned well enough to survive intact the incredible shock wave of the ground burst that took out SPACECOM Central. There was no practical way to damage them, and no need with the orbiter destroyed.

What remained in the last few seconds of the waning window was to show the price of defying Chairman Maximov.

The mirrors stopped again, focused on the collection of prefab buildings and makeshift shacks that housed the families of Vandenberg personnel, as well as the off-duty shifts. The solar accumulator supplied power to the lasing element. An invisible spear lanced earthward.

When the window closed, Mallory turned away from his scope. His face was drained of color, greenish beneath his sideburns. His hands were trembling.

Hocevar smiled like the death mask of an impaled man. "Congratulations, Dr. Mallory. You are an exemplary killer."

"No!" Sylvie Braestrop turned on him, fists clenched, eyes

hot and wide. "He's not a killer! He's a great man." In her excitement, her magnetic slippers lost their grip on the control room's deck, and she floated to the end of her meter-long safety tether.

"All great men have been great killers, Dr. Braestrop," Hocevar said in his quiet hiss.

"No!" the little girl screamed, squirming away from Billy McKay's outstretched hand. "No! *I won't go without Fluffy!*"

Fluffy, McKay thought. *Fuck* me.

"The godda—uh, the building's about to fall on our heads, little girl. C'mon!"

He made a grab for her. The stupid respirator mask was screwing up his depth perception; he missed. At least he *hoped* that's why he missed. If eight-year-olds were going to get the better of him mano a mano . . .

"*Fluffff*-eeee!" she wailed.

He came after her, tripping over a hassock that was hidden under a layer of brown smoke and falling flat. "Fuck!" he bellowed. "Fluffy'll be fine!"

She faced him with her back pressed against a smoking wall. "You're lying."

Well, you got me there, you little bitch. "Come *on*, little girl. Fluffy'd want you to get away while you got a chance."

She folded her arms. "I'm not leaving without Fluffy."

The flames were rearing in the rafters above his head. Pretty shortly more of them were going to be caving in, like the one he'd pulled her out from under moments ago. Unfortunately this was her terrain, and she knew how to use it to best advantage.

"All right," he said, standing still and trying to look as nonthreatening as humanly possible while keeping ready to jump if the onbase-housing apartment building started falling in on him. "Where do we find this Fluffy?"

McKay strode out the front door with the little girl tucked under his arm. The ceiling fell in behind him with a *whoomp*, sending a reverse shower of sparks into the smoky sky.

The girl was shrieking and wailing and beating on him with tiny fists: "Fluffy! *Fluffy!*"

"Like, what happened to *you*, Billy?" asked Casey, stripped to the waist in the heat of more than the high, merciless sun and leaning momentarily on the handle of a shovel he'd been using to dig at the wreckage of the building next door. "Your face is all scratched up like you ran into some broken glass."

McKay gave him a look of hatred so pure the former fighter jock recoiled. A young woman in a soiled yellow dress, who was probably real cute under the smoke and grime and blood from the the cut across her forehead, came running forward and grabbed the little girl out of McKay's arms.

"Ginny! Are you all right?"

The little girl turned to hit at McKay. "He lost Fluffy!"

"Like fuck I did."

"Where is she?"

Wordlessly he turned. A tiny gray-and-white kitten was stuck to him right between his shoulder blades, all four sets of needle kitten claws sunk through his coveralls. Like his buddies, he had shucked out of his Kevlar before pitching into rescue operations.

The cat took only a small area of McKay's skin along as it went gratefully into its mistress's arms. When McKay opened his eyes, he found himself surrounded by a forest of muzzle-brakes.

"Awright," he said, "I admit it. I killed Cock Robin. Slap the cuffs on me."

Dabbing at an angry-looking burn on his right cheek, Sam Sloan stared in puzzlement at the Security Patrol detachment in their blue berets. "What's the matter?"

A pudgy figure thrust through. "You're to leave the base immediately," Major Boyd said. "General's orders. I *told* you I could make you leave, McKay."

McKay's right fist caught Boyd smack in the center of his nose, which splattered like a tomato dropped off the Transamerica Pyramid. He went straight down with McKay on top of him shrugging off blows from the measly collapsible stocks of the SPs' CAR-15s. He had his hands locked on Boyd's throat, and the major's round face was going a most satisfactory black when some of the Blue Berets remembered they had nightsticks and began to play "Inna Gadda Da Vida" on McKay's head.

"Here! Stop all this! Stop it at once."

The drumroll stopped. Boyd reared onto his knees as the SPs fell back. "Shoot him. Shoot him!"

Charging handles clacked like sticks along a picket fence. "No! Hold it! I forbid you to shoot."

It was General Ebersole. Wimp or not, he hadn't lost the bark of command. Thank God.

"They were resisting your orders," Boyd whined.

"You brought this disaster upon us, McKay," Ebersole said. "We appreciate your efforts on our behalf, but they hardly atone for what you've done. Major Boyd was carrying out my command. You are to leave the base at once. If you return, you will be shot on sight."

Major Boyd smirked triumphantly. Past his shoulder McKay saw Filson, face frozen in a look of shock and shame.

McKay laughed. Boyd and Ebersole stared at him as if he'd lost his mind.

"Don't you see, General?" he said, climbing unsteadily to his feet and wiping blood from his eyes. "The Boy here sold us out. He's the one who brought this down on your heads. He told Chairman Max's little helpers we were coming—"

"General! Don't listen to him, General! He's lying!"

Ebersole was shaking his head sadly. "I expected more of you. Trying to escape your moral responsibility for this slaughter of innocents by blackening the name of a brother officer . . . Gentlemen, show them to the gate."

McKay woke up with a nudge in the ribs and a light in his eyes. Usually when he got awakened suddenly his reaction was violent. This set of stimuli produced quite a different response: he tried to remember where he'd landed in the brig *this* time. Modesto? Bakersfield? Dago? He knew by the smell that it wasn't anywhere in the Med.

His eyes got used to the light enough to show him some details of his surroundings. He wasn't in slam at all. He was

in the bedroom he'd been lent at Morgenstern's San Luis
Obispo HQ, with all the woodsy Sierra Club prints on the
walls, and not one naked woman in the bunch. What was
wrong with those people?

Morgenstern's beaky face was hovering up in the light.
"Sorry to disturb you, Lieutenant," he said without any ev-
idence of regret. "You have a visitor."

"Say what?" He sat up, rubbing at his eyes.

A woman was standing next to the bed, hands on hips. She
had on a photojournalist's jacket, and her shiny black hair
hung in a long, thick braid over one shoulder. Her eyes were
Chinese. The way her tight jeans fit her, she looked like an
ideal item to remedy the aesthetic deficiency in the nature
scenes.

"I'm Antoinette Lee," the woman said. "So you're the
schmucks who came for the Blueprints. What the hell took
you so long?"

CHAPTER
NINETEEN ————————————

"So why didn't you ever tell anybody you were in on this Blueprint launch thing?" McKay asked.

Lee glanced at him sideways from behind the controls of the Beechcraft and laughed. "Hey, what a great idea, huh? I'm part of this big, top-drawer, cross-your-heart-and-hope-to-die secret deal, and you're wondering why I didn't like rush out and share it with the first person I met? 'Hey there, Chairman Max, don't tell anybody, but I'm part of the Blueprint for Renewal. Isn't that just the *greatest—*' "

"Okay, okay, don't wear your arm out rubbing it on thick. Besides, you could of told Morgenstern. He was your boss. Hell, he helped put Project Blueprint together."

"Yeah. Like I knew that. They told me not to tell anybody, and after they got through telling me what would happen to me if I did, I decided to humor them, you know? Besides, it's *your* job to find *us.*"

McKay grunted and settled down in his seat with his arms folded across his enormous chest. He'd had to pull rank to get Casey to quit jabbering about flying and let him have the front seat. Now he was wondering if it was worth it. *How come we never meet any girls who aren't butch anymore?* he wondered.

Below them, the Bay Area was a tangle of urban junk gleaming in the morning sun, strewn around a lumpy crescent of blue water.

"Real hellhole down there," Lee remarked, glancing down. "People who survived seem to think the One-Day War was meant as a personal insult. Effsees didn't lighten up their outlook much."

"I hope we don't have engine failure."

She laughed. "We won't," she said with serene assurance. "I preflighted them myself."

"Okay," McKay said, "then I hope somebody didn't put a *bomb* in the goddam plane, okay? I do not feel too secure in the friendly skies these days."

"This isn't Washington, Billy," Casey said, leaning forward in the seat behind. Toni Lee just laughed again.

"I can't believe it," Casey said for about the fifteenth time. "A combat-trained aviator driving a *truck*."

She flipped an insincere little shrug. "Hey, the good doctor doesn't need any full-time pilots yet, and I'm pretty fair with a big rig. If I play my cards right, maybe one day he'll need an air force. Till then I have to make do with the occasional flying fix."

She glanced back at Casey, and the pathetic look they shared almost made McKay bust out laughing.

The Guardians had set out bright and early that morning from the little municipal airport at San Luis Obispo. It was quite a change from their earlier visits to the state, when they'd been reduced to scrabbling around among the ruins and hollow-cheeked survivors, dodging Effsees and doctrinaire leftists. He remembered an earlier run they'd made in the opposite direction, from near the Bay Area to L.A., in a ragged little flotilla of sailboats, battling pirates and with Geoff van Damm's captive hydrogen bomb awaiting them in Disneyland. Even if he remained a little leery of flying, McKay could definitely appreciate the difference in style now.

Maybe the country is comin' back together a little bit. Maybe we're making some kind of difference, after all.

There were clear differences in Doc Morgenstern's style too. They hadn't forgotten when they were first trying to track down the man who seemed to be bent on rebuilding California all by himself if he had to. In those days the Israeli-born paratrooper and tank-brigade commander turned economist had been perfectly satisfied to make his rounds on the back of a donkey scrounged from somewhere. Now he had at his disposal houses with hot tubs and cellars full of wine, and semis, and a comprehensive communications and intelligence-gathering network staffed by underage electronics wizards who thought the most barbaric aftereffect of the war was interrupting their supplies of Pop Tarts and Nacho-flavored Doritos, and a small fleet of airplanes with foxy but mean little Chinese chickadees to fly the beasts.

They had left their three companions from New Mexico behind to enjoy the hot tubs and hospitality of Morgenstern's main base of operations. They didn't seem to be in a hurry to go anywhere, besides which some old buddy of theirs seemed to have turned up working for Dr. J, so they could content themselves getting caught up on two years' worth of gossip and not getting in the way. Morgenstern had even started making noises about finding a use for them. But then, he could find a use for *anybody*.

"Oh, *wow*," Casey Wilson breathed. "It looks just like a set from *The Guns of Navarone*."

Freeman Gilchrist smiled. He was a little taller than Tom Rogers, broader built, dark in the hair and pale in the eyes, with a bearded lantern jaw and something of a limp. He wore a gray-and-burgundy cardigan sweater against the Northern California sea breeze.

It was a decidedly nippy kind of breeze. They stood on a shelf of rock in a tiny cove somewhere on the redwood coast south of Crescent City, so protected by rocky cliffs that loomed on three sides, leaving only a narrow inlet for the sea, that the sun must only penetrate its interior when it was due west or directly overhead. Which it wasn't.

What drew the outburst from Casey—as well as admiring whistles from Sloan and McKay, and even a nod from Tom—was the way gigantic steel shutters had retracted to either side to reveal a large well-lit facility set into the cliff face at the waterline. To McKay it actually looked more like the landing bay on the Death Star, but he could catch Casey's drift.

"*The Guns of Navarone* is appropriate," Gilchrist said. "This was, once upon a time, a coastal defense battery in the Second World War. We understand there was a natural cave formation of some sort, which must have been the reason they picked the place, since the guns couldn't have had much of a field of fire."

He gestured with his gnarled, silver-headed cane. "Shall we repair inside where it's warm?"

They trooped after him along a narrow, spray-slippery trail and into the hidden chamber. The shutters ground to behind them as they entered.

"Don't seem very large for a vehicle-assembly area," McKay remarked, remembering the giant white cubes he'd seen on TV and at Vandenberg.

"The StarVan was intended to be a smaller, more economical, quicker turnaround version of the shuttle."

"Ah," said Sloan, "I see. So when the newer, more cost-effective generations of NASA shuttles came along, there was no reason to continue the project."

Gilchrist's mouth tightened, but he kept his tone light and easy. "Not at all, Commander."

"The later shuttles were even more heavily subsidized than the original ones," Toni Lee remarked from the back of the pack. "That's why the jerk media were able to pass them off as more economical."

"As you can see, gentlemen—I exempt Commander Lee, who is fully familiar with our setup here—our orbiter was not built to have the cargo capacity of a railway car."

He pointed again. There it was, a gleaming, white little arrowhead with upturned wing tips. It was, in fact, a great deal smaller than the standard shuttle, which was a lot bigger than most people thought. This was more the size of a school bus than a freight car, and more streamlined than the late, lamented orbiter at Vandenberg. Technicians in blue and orange jumpsuits stood by, watching the Guardians with interest.

"Why down here on the water?" McKay wanted to know. "I mean, it's easier to keep secret, I can see that. But how were you gonna *launch* the damn thing?"

"We were developing a technique of water launching that required much less by way of support machinery than gantry launch. Orbiter and boosters are lowered from the surface, using the really gigantic elevators left over from the days this was a big-gun battery, and assembled in here. Then we would tow them out to sea in a sort of big padded flotation collar and fire them off."

" 'Would?' " Sloan asked.

Gilchrist shrugged. "Come into my office, if you will. We'll have a drink and I'll explain the situation to you."

"It was the government," said Gilchrist's assistant, Anne Dowling. She was a narrow, nervous-looking black woman with big glasses, a high dome of forehead, and extremely light skin who stood with her arms crossed under her breasts and her back to a filing cabinet. "They kept us from becoming operational. They were *all* that kept us from it."

Stacked in a chair in his usual unmilitary slouch, Casey looked puzzled. "But I thought the government helped you set up here, like, as part of Project Blueprint."

"Lieutenant," said Gilchrist, seated behind the enameled metal desk in his cramped and garishly lit office, "no true space enthusiast was ever happy with the way NASA handled space exploration: one political extravaganza after another, mostly show devoid of substance, whether it was sending golfers to the moon or giant, lethally jury-rigged buses into orbit. We would have made a deal with the devil to take some *real* steps beyond the gravity well."

He sat back in his creaking wheeled chair. "Eventually that's what we did."

"For all the rhetoric of the Reagans and Wild Bill Lowells," Dowling said, "the government was never pleased with the thought of any *private* space development. NASA never

made any secret of hating the whole idea. Originally, private
space exploration was held back by the capital-gains tax
structure and FTC regulations, which made it difficult to cap-
italize a long-term, high-risk venture. Then NASA was made
the space regulatory agency and was in position to virtually
choke us off.''

"What finished 'em," Lee said, sipping black coffee from
an enameled metal cup, "was insurance, of all things. Feds
made the insurance requirements for would-be private space
operations so high, they had to fold their hands.''

Gilchrist nodded. "So when representatives of the government arrived in our offices literally as the finance company
was repossessing our furniture, and offered a way we could
continue our work, is it any wonder we said yes?''

"Sold our souls," Dowling said.

"Yes. But you agreed, Anne.''

"Yeah. And I've hated myself ever since.''

"Excuse me," Sloan said. "Do you mean this wasn't your
original base of operations?''

"Oh, no," Gilchrist said. "Project Blueprint gave us the
site, and capital to build it up as we required. They were
quite generous—off-budget, you know.''

"Hey," McKay growled, "paid the bills, you know?''

"Yes. And I should not bite the hand that fed us, I know.''
Gilchrist put an arm over the back of his chair. "But mere
curiosity didn't bring you here.''

"It's Cygnus, isn't it?'' Dowling asked.

McKay raised his eyebrows. "What? Did everybody know
about this but us?''

"Everybody knows about the good old Star Wars laser by
now, that's for sure," Lee said. "Or they haven't been tuned
into KFSU like good little born-agains.''

'I'm born again,' said Rogers gently.

"Ah, but I didn't say born-again *what*, Lieutenant. You're
a human being. Forrie's faithful strike me as something you'd
be likely to shake out of your boot on a camping trip to Death
Valley.''

"We always knew there was some kind of skullduggery
going on with Cygnus," Dowling said heatedly. "Especially

when they started denying top astronomers access to it, on the grounds that the satellite passed over sensitive military facilities and they wouldn't sign loyalty oaths.''

"So, yeah, that's what brought us here. We need to get up to the satellite and kick some ass. We gotta do it in a hell of a hurry, too; been reports coming in since last night about civil disorder all over the country. For a would-be benefactor of humanity, old Chairman Max wasn't real shy about advertising how he greased a few hundred noncombatants at Vandenberg.''

"The Effsees must be stopped," Gilchrist agreed. He folded his hands on his desktop and looked at them intently. "I only wish we could help you do it."

CHAPTER
TWENTY

"This is never gonna work," Billy McKay said, peering nervously forward through the Lexan windshield.

"You always say that, Billy," Casey Wilson said from the pilot's seat of the cargo plane with the StarVan shackled to its back, "and it always does."

"You actually think we're gonna get away with this?"

Casey grinned. "Probably not, man. But, like you always say, what the hey?"

Small the StarVan mini-shuttle undoubtedly was, and Billy McKay was willing to concede that it was economical as well—what the hey, right? But even he knew the damn thing couldn't clamber up to orbit all by its lonesome.

The STS facility belonged to a decidedly experimental category of Blueprint components. Like Starshine in Wolf Bayou, it was a process that was, with luck, continuing toward a goal when it was incorporated into the Blueprint, not a finished asset. Starshine had made important breakthroughs since the One-Day War.

So might STS. Except for one little problem.

The Project Blueprint control officer insisted that STS abandon its established suppliers when it was incorporated into the Blueprint. That meant starting over from scratch with Blueprint-approved contractors. With the country fighting heavy undeclared wars throughout the Mediterranean basin and gearing up for the title bout with the Russians, getting materials and assembly-line time wasn't any too easy.

What all that meant was the boosters had never been delivered. And the Effsees had gone and blown up the plant where they were manufactured.

"We've stayed here basically to keep the flame alive, though there's always more calculations and simulations to run," was how Gilchrist explained it. "We always hoped something would happen to let us get back on track, but, candidly, none of us had much idea what that might be."

Oh, yeah.

McKay's first reaction had been an intense desire to strangle Toni Lee, which he'd periodically wanted to do anyway. Gilchrist explained that she had not led them out here on a deliberate wild-goose chase.

"She was a technical adviser for several years before the war," he said, "and we had promised her the first shuttle mission. Because the Blueprint wanted us to run on a strict need-to-know basis, she was never kept informed as to our actual status here. We would give her warning when we began mission prep; that was the arrangement."

So what Antionette Lee hadn't "needed to know" was that the StarVan orbiter was a large, pleasingly shaped paperweight. It was time for America to spread cheeks for Chairman Max. *Except* . . .

Except boosters and tanks aplenty still existed unharmed at Vandenberg. The humanitarians on board Cygnus had been so eager to start sizzling women and children that they never bothered with them. Without an orbiter the people on the ground couldn't do them any harm, anyway, right?

Of course, there was the problem that General Ebersole had unconditionally refused to help the Guardians, or even permit them on base. "Shot on sight" was how he put it;

yes, indeed. And you had Maggie Connoly on the radio every hour telling the country what an incompetent doob President Jeff was, and rioters all across the formerly United States who didn't want to be the next orbitally induced crispy critters.

It was clearly time, as Otter said in *Animal House*—one of McKay's favorite movies of all time, along with *Deep Inside Vanessa del Rio*—it was time for somebody to make a really stupid, futile gesture. And Billy McKay was clearly the man to do it—with a little help from his friends.

They had one more tiny little problem: General Beaumont of Edwards had announced his intention to support Dr. Connoly to the fullest extent possible. His command would resist to the utmost any attempt to interfere with the Cygnus earth-orbital station.

And he had an air force to back him up.

"You surprised the hell out of me, Casey," McKay said.

Casey had the radio headset pulled down over his inevitable tour cap—this one said RAMONES, which made McKay kind of wonder about him—chewing some scarfed gum and just bopping along with the morning sunlight shining on his face as if this were what he'd most like to be doing in the whole world. Which flying pretty much was.

And the plane was a technological wonder—Casey had told him so himself. It was one of these damn ass-backward New Age jobs with the propellers in the rear and the tail plane up in the nose. It had as much lift as the C-130 they'd lost over the Staked Plains, and a shorter takeoff roll and higher top speed and lower fuel use and blah, blah, blah.

What it *wasn't* was a fighter. Especially not the sole, sexy F-16, just like the one Casey used to fly, remaining on duty at Vandenberg.

Casey pulled one earpiece aside. "What do you mean, Billy?"

"Not taking the combat side of this gig. I thought you'd kill to get back into the cockpit of a Falcon."

Casey shrugged. "It's not that easy flying this beast with the StarVan on top. And this is, like, the key to the whole thing. We bend the orbiter on landing, we're kind of out of—''

''Altitude, airspeed, and ideas. Yeah. I know. But still, a *broad*?''

''We all agreed on this—us and Dr. Morgenstern. There's, like, sound psychological reasons for this—''

''All of which are bullshit.''

The former fighter jock laughed. ''Yeah. I guess so. But you didn't come up with any better ideas, and meanwhile we have thirty-two hours before Cygnus is back in the position to hit Vandenberg again. And the country is, like, splitting at the seams.''

''Don't give me too much good news. My central nervous system can't handle it.''

''Oh. Then I probably shouldn't tell you we're about to enter the fringe of what we figure is Edwards' radar coverage, then, should I?''

''Casey, you're weird.''

''Anything you say, Billy.''

McKay peered into the clear blue sky ahead, as if expecting to see the dark shapes of intercepting Edwards fighters above the horizon. ''I hope the others don't screw up their end,'' he said.

''Read my lips, bobo. It overheated. Got that?''

The trooper's eyes flickered beneath the Kevlar brim of his Fritz helmet, from the steam pouring out of the open radiator of the white Maverick to the sawed-off guy with the square cleft chin and the shock of blond hair facing him beside it in the road.

''I dunno. This is a restricted area. What were you doing out here?''

''Driving *around*. Look. See that sign there?'' He pointed a blunt finger at the high fence topped with rolls of German knife wire.

The soldier's lips moved briefly, then his eyes lit with a triumphant gleam. ''Yeah. It says, RESTRICTED AREA. KEEP OUT. Just like I'm telling you—''

''So, don't you think that implies the area on the *other* side is what's restricted? And that the law-abiding citizens of the formerly great state of California are therefore perfectly entitled to have breakdowns *outside* it?''

The soldier stuck out his lower lip. ''Yeah, but I still wanna know what you were doing pokin' around—''

He didn't get any further, because there was a *thunk* from the general vicinity of the back of his head. His knees folded beneath him, and he was loudly sick on the short blond guy's tennis shoes.

''Ack!'' the blond guy exclaimed, leaping back out of range like a startled cat. ''Ag! You twisted maniac, what do you think you're doing? I had him listening to reason, and you had to go and clock him in the head. What's the matter with you?''

Killer stood behind the barfing soldier, holding the SAW she'd used to slug him at parade rest. ''Don't be such a crybaby, Sacker. We don't have all day.''

Her gray-blue eyes scanned the terrain on the far side of the controversial fence. It ran mainly to white dunes and green clumps of bush, which concealed their stretch of road from view from the inhabited areas of the base. No sign of movement.

She turned to the Sacker, who now stood on the shoulder kicking his feet in the sand to soak up the puke. ''Get this clown tied up. We've got a diversion to create.''

Grumbling and bitching, the Sacker obeyed. Scooter appeared out of the weeds on the other side of the road carrying an M-79 grenade launcher. ''What's all the commotion? Is everything all right?''

''Yeah, babe, everything's fine. This bozo sentry stumbled along, and Sacker was trying to show what a brain he was by arguing about how many angels could dance on his pin head.''

''Very funny,'' Sacker muttered.

''Where's Skids?'' Killer asked.

''I don't know. I think he wandered off to take a leak.''

''Great,'' Sacker said, rolling the groggy and now gagged troopie behind a bush with his shoe. ''We're ready to rock and roll, and that buffoon Skids is off with his dick in his hand. Just exquisite.''

Killer put the hand that held her cigarette to her ear. "Hold on. Toni and the G-men are in position. This is it."

Sacker reached in the Maverick's back window for his own M-79. Skids came slogging out of the ditch on the far side of the road and did a frantic little dance step.

"What the fuck happened to you?" Killer asked.

Skids blushed. "I, uh, got caught in my zipper."

"Jesus. You got your piece, or did that get stuck in your zipper too?" Skids held up his stubby grenade launcher.

"Right," Killer said. "Remember, CS only. These are good guys—until they start getting too close for comfort."

"Yeah, yeah," Sacker said, fishing a trashcan-shaped tear-gas grenade out of a pocket of his denim vest. "We've been over all this before. We should be long gone by the time anybody starts nosing around out this way."

"That's the drill," Killer said. She angled the M-249 off in the general direction of the Pacific Ocean and triggered a burst one-handed. "Let's hope it works out that way."

"Whoa!" Seahawk said, straightening up from beneath the leading edge of the wing, where he'd been inspecting the actuators that automatically altered the wing's camber during flight. "What the heck was that?"

Otis pointed off at an angle toward the runway shimmering like a laketop in the hot morning sun. Clouds of white smoke were billowing up near the perimeter.

"Gunfire," Otis said. "Grenades or mortar rounds going off, too, looks like."

"Shoot. That's all we need." Most personnel not urgently needed elsewhere were still involved in cleaning up after the laser attack two days ago.

Otis frowned and scratched his chin, which, in spite of endless write-ups and demerits, he was unable to keep alto-gether stubble-free. "Wonder if they're gonna tow this baby into revetments?"

"Whoa, they better. It's the only one they got left."

Neither man made a move toward finding cover himself. Whatever was going down was doing so a couple of klicks away. In the days since the war they'd learned to recognize the kind of danger that could reach them at this range, and they'd seen no sign of such yet.

"Maybe not," Otis said. "Look."

Again Seahawk looked where he was pointing, which was this time back toward the hangar, from which a little cart was approaching with two mechanics and a flight-suited pilot aboard.

"That's funny. They never scrambled for a ground attack before." The F-16's scheduled patrol wasn't till that afternoon.

"Always a first time," said Otis, thrusting his hands deep in the pockets of his coveralls.

He started back to the plane. Seahawk clutched his arm.

"Wait a second," Seahawk said. "There's something funny going on."

"You been out in the sun too long."

"No, really. I ain't never seen these dudes before, and, dang, that's a short little pilot. Dang."

Otis was giving him his skeptical look. The shorter, stockier man tried to pull away, but Seahawk got a fresh grip on his sleeve.

"Wait, my man, wait. Check it out—the pilot's a *woman*."

More explosives were cracking off in the distance. Otis glared at his buddy as if wondering whether he should cold-cock him and go looking for a psychiatric officer.

Instead, something he caught in the corner of his eye made him turn. And stare. A cute little Chinese girl in a flight suit was walking toward them with a helmet tucked under her arm. She gave them a bright smile.

Belatedly Otis noticed that the man in the cart's passenger seat was pointing some kind of submachine gun with a real fat barrel on it right at him.

"Morning, boys," Sam Sloan said. "Mind if we borrow your airplane?"

CHAPTER
TWENTY-ONE ─────────────

"General," the intercom squawked, *"there's a message coming in for you."*

Ebersole stood at the window staring out—his staff had insisted on replacing it with salvaged glass after the war, though he personally felt it more important to see his personnel's living quarters reglazed. He realized there was potential danger in standing here like this, but whatever kind of attack was taking place, it was happening far away and seemed small and localized. Security units were headed for the area the fire was coming from, and Major Boyd assured him the attackers would be rounded up shortly.

Still, he didn't feel he had a lot of leisure for chitchat. "Tell them to call me back later," he instructed.

"But it's Lieutenant McKay of the Guardians. He says he's in an airplane headed this way."

The general frowned, walked to his desk. "Patch him through, by all means."

"General, this is Billy McKay."

"So I gather. I warned you of the consequences should you attempt to enter this facility again."

"*Listen, Jack, I got orders from the president himself. I also got an orbital vehicle strapped to the back of this plane. We are going to launch it using your fuel and your boosters.*"

Ebersole felt alternately hot and cold. "I'll have you shot down."

"*You're gonna have to stand in line. Your good buddy General Beaumont's just scrambled four fighters to smoke us. If your eyes're still good, you might just get to see the show.*"

"Are you out of your mind? A slow, overloaded cargo plane—you'll be massacred!" Despite his own professed intentions, he was shocked.

"*Maybe not. I think we got an escort on the way about . . . now.*"

Ebersole heard the distinctive rising roar of a jet taking off. He spun back toward the window to see Vandenberg's last fighter leap into the sky.

"You son of a bitch!" he shouted. "You think stealing my airplane's going to make me help you? You *are* nuts."

"*Maybe so, General. But I'm a soldier too. I got my orders, and I'm gonna do everything in my power to carry them out. McKay out.*"

The connection broke. Ebersole was still holding his head in one hand and shaking it when the intercom said, "Sir, now we have a call coming in from our airplane."

"Put him on."

"*General Ebersole,*" the new voice said, "*this is Lieutenant Commander Antoinette Lee, United States Navy. I've commandeered your aircraft on direct authorization of the president of the United States of America.*"

He stared blindly at the framed photographs of his predecessor and his exploits. *A woman?*

"*I will try my best to return it to you as soon as possible, and in the best possible condition.*"

"Young woman, are you aware that there are four fighters being vectored toward you on ground-controlled intercept?"

"*Yes, sir. I guess that means you should root real hard for me, if you want your plane back intact. Lee out.*"

"They'll get them," a nasal voice said behind him.

He turned around. "Chris! You gave me quite a scare, my boy." He wondered vaguely why the major wasn't out overseeing the base's defense directly.

Boyd's face was flushed. "They'll shoot those bastards down, sir. Don't worry about that!"

"Whatever happens, those are brave men. And a very brave young woman," Ebersole said, almost to himself. His eyes strayed toward the tiny snapshot in the unadorned frame he kept on his desk, turned so visitors would never see it.

"They're a menace. Don't forget the devastation they caused."

Something in his security chief's manner gave the general pause. "Chris," he said softly, "did you have anything to do with informing the FSE of the Guardians' visit?"

Boyd bit his lip. "Any actions I have taken, I was only following your lead, General. I would never do anything to jeopardize the interests of this country—or you personally, sir."

Ebersole sighed. He suddenly looked even older.

"I see," he said.

"So Beaumont launched," Toni Lee said from the radio. *"Figures. Bastard always did suck Effsee ass."*

"We got the word from Morgenstern," McKay said. "He has spies watching Edwards, and I think he's into their radio traffic too. They're ten minutes from intercepting us."

He glanced sideways at Casey. "Sure you can handle them, Commander?"

"Piece of cake. Remember, if anything happens to either one of us, there goes my chance of getting into space."

"Ha! Fat chance. That's one mission you're sitting out, baby."

"I'm nobody's baby, McKay. I've been weaned, which is more than I can say for you, the way you're always sucking that cigar."

McKay took his unlit cigar from his mouth, stared at it in outrage, and stuck it defiantly back in.

"Now quit trying to discourage me from doing all I can to save your fat butt, McKay. I got work to do."

Toni Lee's whole body was tingling. It felt good to be back in a cockpit. She had flown F-16s before and had almost forgotten how sweet they were.

The cargo plane with the orbiter riding piggyback was grunting along at twenty thousand feet. The F-16 was a little climbing beast, so Toni pitched her nose up and fired her up to forty thou. She was a little taken aback by just how fast the little airplane climbed. It was hauling an amazingly light load: no drop tanks, just four missiles, all AIM-9M Sidewinders. She went up like a rocket.

Her radar was giving her noise to the east. That was no surprise. Even though the Edwards fighters were outdated National Guard jobs, they had very modern avionics. The way microelectronic technology had been zipping along the last few years, upgrades were no big deal anymore: You just popped the old module out and popped the new one in, and you were ready to kick the tires and light the fires and *go*.

Likewise the bandits weren't getting much useful on their screens, either. That would not alert them to her presence in all probability; cargo planes could carry cutting-edge ECM kits too.

It was shaping up to be a very basic kind of fight, pilot against pilot, plane against plane. Most of the fancy electronics/counterelectronics/counter-counterelectronics, and so on tended to cancel out. She wasn't carrying regular radar-homing missiles—and guessed the opposition wasn't, either—because she guessed she'd never get a lock. She wasn't carrying the more sophisticated AIM-120s, which you fired and forgot about, because the Effsees had stolen them all from Vandenberg, and she was betting they'd looted Edwards of them too. Her Sidewinder heat-seekers carried nifty logic circuits in their heads to keep from chasing decoy flares, but she also had decoy flares in her dispenser designed to outsmart those circuits—and again, she had to assume the bad guys had similar gear.

She was getting reports in her headset now. Dr. Morgenstern had woken up his whole network for this gig; spotters on the ground were calling in reports on the Edwards flight as it passed over their heads. The observers had no good way to estimate height or speed, but they could tell her which way they were headed, and from the timing and location of reports she could estimate how fast they were moving. The spies at Edwards said there were two F-5s and two Phantoms. When the reports started coming in about two aircraft, she guessed the flight had split and wondered which went high and which low.

It all came back to the old standbys: the tactical advantages of height and surprise, keen eyes, fast reflexes, and cannon at close range. And one of the most maneuverable aircraft in the world.

If only I can keep from being detected for a few more minutes.

"No," General Ebersole said from the window.

"But, General," Boyd whined, "it's our duty to warn the fighters from Edwards that our F-16's been stolen."

"Maybe it is, boy. But I'm no longer quite so sure where my duty lies."

Boyd studied the general's back. He moistened his lips. "Uh, if you'll excuse me, General, I need to attend to a few matters—"

"You'll not leave this room until I give you permission," Ebersole snapped with a harshness Boyd had never heard from him before.

The general turned, his face displaying a mixture of sadness and contempt.

"You might as well sit down and make yourself at home, boy. Circumstances have taken events out of our hands, and that's where I want them to stay for the moment."

She was over the place where State 166 cut the Sierra Madres when she spotted them: two dark-mottled hunchback shapes at thirty-six thousand feet, their course neatly crossing her bows. She pitched the nose up a few more degrees and hit the burners briefly to wring just a hair more height advan-

tage, then banked into a three-gee tactical turn to line up on
their tails.

If either of the pilots or rear-instrument operators noticed
her, their planes showed no signs as she assumed the classic
position for the bounce. They were probably all but mashing
their eyeballs on the windshield in their eagerness to pick out
the grotesquely sexual shape of the orbiter mounted atop the
cargo plane.

Her one concern was that *she* might be the one getting set
up in a tactical sandwich. There were a few turds of cloud
floating between her and the planet, and in the gap between
a couple of those, her eyes caught just a splinter of silver,
then another: two dagger-nosed F-5s at twenty thousand feet,
paralleling their big brothers' course.

"That's it," she said aloud, and put her own nose down.

The Phantoms swelled alarmingly. She activated her heat-
seekers, was rewarded almost instantaneously by the heart-
warming buzz of the annunciator, indicating that the missiles'
infrared eyes had found nice hot exhausts to lock on to.

An electric current was running in her belly. This was the
real thing, this was *it,* the thing she'd aimed her life at so
long ago.

Her stomach was telling her, shoot, *shoot.* But she held on.
Her 9-Mikes didn't smoke, but you didn't know if that flicker
of motion when one came off the rail would snag the peripheral vision of an alert back-seater. If it did, you didn't want
him to call out a warning to his pilot in time to break out of
the missile's path. On the other hand, you didn't want to get
so close that somebody spotted you and broke before you
even fired.

At 2,500 meters range she figured she was crowding her
luck and fired. The missile came off the pylon smoothly and
guided straight for the right-hand Phantom.

With heart-stopping quickness the two enemy aircraft split
in opposite directions. Though she'd been coming up quick
on the minimum range at which the missile could be fired,
she was afraid she'd triggered it too soon.

The Sidewinder corrected and exploded beside the Phantom's tail. Black smoke began to pour from the aircraft, but it still seemed to be under control.

Time for a lightning decision, Toni, she told herself. The F-4E was a tough motherfucker; she couldn't assume one missile hit was going to take the target down. But if she hung with the injured plane, trying to make sure of it, that left the other three free to bore in toward the cargo plane.

Right. That was easy enough. She broke left and followed the other Phantom in a diving turn.

He was managing to keep out of the tracking cone of her Sidewinders. A pretty good trick considering that the Falcon could hold a turn longer and respond quicker then his big Phantom. If they were just in this one on one now, he would be in a world of pain, because sooner or later he'd misjudge and she'd get a lock on his tailpipe.

Or she could close the range and shoot him. Which she didn't dare do just yet. At this stage he *wanted* her to get fascinated with closing and killing him, gambling that while she was concentrating on him, his buddies could climb up and scrape her off his tail. She was holding off committing herself to nailing him, waiting to see if the F-5s did the smart thing, which was to leave their man spinning in the breeze and drive like motherfuckers for the target.

Above her, she caught sight of a polychrome puff as a parachute opened and the Phantom she'd hit came spinning down, drawing a corkscrew of dense black smoke. *Gotcha,* she thought; even if that was meant as a trick, the other guy was fucked, because the F-4 had the spin-recovery characteristics of a brick. *One down.*

And *here* they came. She saw a slim shape climbing toward her fast at two o'clock—just the one, which meant they'd probably split and were up to something cute. Fine—she had a plan in mind for that.

She cranked hard right, right into the bastard, flipping her gunsight to snapshoot mode as she did so. She gave him a quick burst head-on, just to loosen his sphincters, and then they flashed past one another, almost cockpit to cockpit.

Immediately she brought her nose up into a howling vertical climb. She pulled through and fell off into an inverted dive right down the F-5's tailpipe as he was plotting his next cunning move.

She rolled upright. Staying in snapshoot, she gave him a good burst that walked right up the fuselage. He exploded in blinding yellow fire and started to break up before her eyes. The pilot didn't punch out.

CHAPTER
TWENTY-TWO ─────────────

"*Scratch one* kwailo," the radio warbled. "*Tora, Tora, Tora!*"

Casey whooped and pumped his fist in the air. "Two, two, two," he chanted, like a fan at a close basketball game.

McKay looked at him. "You know, *all* you fighter types are pretty weird."

They had been up to something, all right. No sooner had the F-5 come apart than the second one whipped by to Toni's left on pretty much a reciprocal bearing. He had been setting himself up to take her in the ass, but her lightning-quick vertical maneuver had caught him as much by surprise as it had his buddy.

But now things were getting ugly. Even if Phantoms no longer drew big black lines of smoke across the sky—well, unless they were on fire—they were still big, highly visible aircraft. And Toni got a relatively fine view of the surviving F-4E making a beeline for Casey's cargo plane, vaguely visible now in the distance.

"Whale One, this is Renegade," she said into her microphone. "You've got company headed your way."

"Thank you so much for the good news," Billy McKay's voice came back. *"Time to save the whales, or Chairman Max gets to own the world."*

"I'll do my best, Whale One."

She was up against it here, and the bad guys knew it. The F-4E had a lot of speed up from his panic dive, and was making the most of it. Toni had her afterburner cut in, trying frantically to close within Sidewinder range. The problem was, while she was fast enough to overtake the Phantom at this altitude, she was giving the F-5 a clean shot at her tail, plus a grossly expanded heat signature for his IR-tipped missiles to home on.

It was unlikely he could catch her before she got in range of the Phantom. But when she caught the F-4, they would all be getting uncomfortably near the cargo plane with its priceless cargo. Even if she dealt with the Phantom cleanly, she was going to have some tough choices. . . .

"Well, here they come," McKay said, eying the black form of the approaching Phantom. "Why do I feel like something from *The Far Side* when I say that?"

"Well," Casey said brightly, "we know they don't have radar homing missiles."

"Why's that, Mr. Science?"

"They'd have launched them by now."

"Terrific." He glanced at the Phantom again. Was it really getting close enough so he could see the way the wings turned up at the ends, or was that just buried memory from building models of the damn things when he was a kid?

"Casey, don't you want to, like, maneuver or anything?"

"With this thing on top? Be serious, man."

"Then I guess it's a day at the races, and we're betting our lives on China Girl to show."

Without really thinking about it, Toni had been climbing gently. The Phantom, alertly, was doing it, too, but the bigger plane had to spend more energy to climb and therefore couldn't climb as fast as she was without losing speed. Behind her, the F-5 was also in a gradual climb.

At what she judged was the proper instant she dropped the nose and dived into the Phantom for the second half of the yo-yo maneuver. The F-4 began punching out flares but kept its nose aimed straight at the lumbering cargo plane.

"Come on, you bastard," Toni said, "break. *Break.* Save your *life*, you asshole."

But he didn't. He was sacrificing himself, doing what was known as "dragging" her for his buddy to jump. That his buddy couldn't catch up quickly enough to save his ass wasn't making any difference, and Toni felt grudging admiration for him. What his rear-seater thought was another matter, of course.

She fired a missile, knowing the son of a bitch wouldn't even try to dodge—because to do so would be to take himself out of the fight long enough to permit her to turn on his comrade. And he didn't dodge, but that didn't matter, because the fancy decoy-rejection logics in her seeker head decided to get stupid and go blow up a goddam flare.

The Phantom was fast approaching missile range of the cargo plane. He would get a Sidewinder off long before she closed to cannon range of him. She ground her teeth and fired a second missile.

This one went into his tail pipe and tumbled him. His rear-seater came popping out before the missile even hit. The pilot didn't come out, as far as Toni saw.

There was no time to confirm whether he'd made the ultimate sacrifice. The bad guys knew all about how she could pitch straight up and give them problems now, but she did it again, anyway. Among other things, it was a speed-losing maneuver—and the very last thing in all the world she wanted to do was to zip past the cargo plane, putting it between herself and the shark-lean enemy fighter.

She came out of the vertical climb headed straight for the F-5. At long range they both fired at once—he two missiles, she her last remaining one. She began to unload a few flares of her own.

She could see the Sidewinders headed for her, twin needles

that looked black against the sky even though they were painted white. Their smokeless propellant charge was already burned out; they were running on pure momentum. Unfortunately they ran very fast.

Her last advantage over the F-5—hair-fine and maybe illusory—was that she could now afford to flinch. A break turn on her part would tend to keep her between hunter and quarry, where she wanted to be. For him to break would be to sheer off, away from his target.

He did, anyway. "Chicken!" she exulted, hurling her machine right and down at the last split second before impact. She saw her missile flash off. Her enemy hadn't gotten all the way clear.

She dodged one Sidewinder but not the other. There was a flash beneath the F-16's belly. She felt an impact in her leg, felt the little plane shudder and slew halfway round, skidding across the sky but not quite falling into a fatal tumble.

She was upright, and for the moment under control. A mile away she saw her opponent limping on a tattered right wing, trying to turn onto an interception heading with the cargo plane.

She turned her nose toward him, thrust forward the throttle. The plane began to vibrate, and the board was a shout of red in her eyes. It didn't matter. She'd ram the son of a bitch it she had to.

He saw her coming and tried to dodge. Late, too late. Her 20-mm tracers splashed right into his cockpit. The F-5 was falling like a leaf as she hurtled past.

Her engine stopped. For a moment the world seemed totally silent, and then she became aware of the whistling of the wind, the crackling of fire, the thousand almost organic pings and pops and cracks as the little aircraft, stressed and punished beyond endurance, began to fall apart.

"All right, McKay, you've got clear sailing from here. How about that, Casey? Did I measure up?"

"Sierra Hotel, Toni. Are you all right?"

"Nothing modern science can't cure, as we used to say. At least, I don't think so. General, if you're listening, I'm sorry about your airplane. I really tried to get it back to you.

"Lee out. And I do mean *out.*"

• • •

The dogfight had carried into view of Vandenberg. Despite the threat of ground attack—firing on the perimeter had long since stopped, anyway—everyone not immediately needed to do what they were doing had wandered outside to watch.

General Ebersole stood out by the runway in front of his office with a crowd of people around him. Somebody had a radio tuned to the F-16's frequency, and the crowd cheered Lee's cries of victory more loudly each time. They gasped when she was hit—she was being a lot more talkative than she realized—and then broke out into a frenzy when the final F-5 fell.

When Toni's parachute blossomed in the sky, the mob let go a single pent-up breath in relief. Tears were shining on General Ebersole's cheeks. He wasn't alone.

"What did they say?" McKay demanded, unsure he'd heard right.

"Vandenberg says we're cleared to land, Billy."

McKay slumped back in his seat. "Well, I'll be dipped in shit. They actually went for it."

He should have been cheering and hollering in celebration, but it felt as if he'd drained into his boots. All he could think about was what was yet to come.

A few moments later he sat up straight. "What the fuck?" he said. "Is that somebody on the *runway*?"

Major Boyd had had enough. *He* knew what was right, even if no one else did. The general would realize he was doing the right thing, once he came to his senses.

And even if he didn't . . . there were others in the world who would appreciate what he was doing, people placed much higher than the officer commanding the shattered remnant of a military base.

He knelt squarely in the middle of the runway, bringing the RPG-16 to his shoulder. The Russian antitank grenade launcher had been left behind by the retreating Effsees. It could punch a hole through a tank. It would surely suffice to take out a cargo plane.

The bizarre doubled shape of aircraft and orbiter grew larger until it filled the sky, and Boyd could see the two damned Guardians gesticulating at him from behind the windshield. He heard the crowd screaming as from a great way off. He ignored the noise.

He smiled. His finger tightened on the trigger. He couldn't miss—

White-hot agony lanced through his chest. He fell. The launcher fired, blowing a crater in the pavement twenty meters away.

General Nathan Ebersole handed the CAR-15 back to a shocked Blue Beret. "Thank you for the loan, son. I should have done that two years ago."

A great winged shadow swept across the motionless body of Major Boyd, and the plane and its cargo touched safely down.

CHAPTER
TWENTY-THREE ─────────

Billy McKay had been in some scaly situations in his life. He had been bombed, strafed, shot at. He had jumped out of airplanes, been blown out of helicopters, had airplanes blow up when he was riding in them. He had even been tied in a ground-burst crater, left to fry slowly from radiation.

But he had never before found himself lying on top of a giant firecracker waiting for the fuse to be lit. It wasn't a comfortable experience.

He never had been one to see his whole life passing before his eyes. But now he kept catching glimpses of the recent past:

Like watching Lee's missile and the one her final opponent had launched both flashing off on target, and wondering if that was going to be enough. If the F-5 came out and the Fighting Falcon didn't, he and Case could just kiss their butts good-bye. . . .

Like late last night, trying to work out the last-minute details of the world's most ad hoc space mission by kerosene lantern in one of the commissaries. And realizing they would *never* work out a lot of the details. They had to launch early the next day, before Cygnus came back within laser reach of the base. Even if they managed to protect the orbiter, Cygnus could fry their gantries, and no matter what mode of launch StarVan was originally intended for the Air Force boosters to which it had to be shackled weren't designed for water lift-off.

"Okay," Toni Lee said, tapping a light pen on her notebook computer. She looked especially foxy in the yellow-amber lantern glow, especially since she kept getting this big smile on her face whenever she remembered the day's events. The chunk she'd taken in her leg had buried itself in muscle and done little damage. "How much zero-gee training do you guys have?"

The Guardians looked at each other.

"I've been in free-fall," Casey said.

"Yeah. Of course you have. But nobody's had any training in moving and working under weightless conditions?"

The silence was thunderous. It had finally happened: The Guardians had found something their training hadn't covered.

"Well," Toni said, looking thoughtful, "you guys are reasonably well coordinated and in good physical shape—"

"Casey and I read lots of science fiction, if that's any help," Sloan said. "We know what it *ought* to be like."

McKay put his hands over his face.

"Well, I guess it can't hurt that you already know stuff like, if you start moving in one direction, you keeping moving that way unless something stops you. Otherwise . . ." She shrugged. "Some of their people are liable to have some experience in orbit, but neither side did much about training people for close combat in space. Everybody was too embarrassed."

She stopped. A giggle bubbled out of her, and then laughter came spilling out, so long and loud and enthusiastic that McKay thought she'd gone right over the top. He looked wildly at his companions. *Should I slap her? Little bitch'll take my hand off at the elbow.*

"Quit looking at me as if I've gone over the high wall into

bananaland, McKay,'' she managed to spit out between fresh bursts of laughter. ''Something just occurred to me: You sad fuckers *have* to take me along. I'm the only one who knows how to mount the goddam laser shield. *If I don't go, Cygnus X-1's gonna blast you out of the sky before you get within a hundred miles!*''

The memory bits kept bubbling up as McKay waited.

—Taking leave of their companions from New Mexico that morning before boarding the van for the launchpad.

''Thanks for the presents, man,'' Casey Wilson said. McKay actually tried not to look skeptical, but it beat the ass off him what use the funky going-away gifts the New Mexicans had given them could be. But the mass-raising capacity of even the little StarVan was substantial enough that they could load on all the personal gear they cared to boost.

''I sure hope you two stay together,'' he told Killer. ''I never met anybody more suited to being Mrs. Trash in all my life.''

''Fuck you very much, McKay.''

''You have a nice day too.''

''You ready, McKay?'' Toni Lee called from her acceleration couch up in the nose as Casey brought the countdown on home.

''No,'' he said.

''*Zero,*'' Casey chanted. ''Tower, we have ignition.''

And a volcano was going off right under Billy McKay's personal butt.

Being launched into orbit wasn't so bad, Billy McKay reflected. It was sort of like being a professional wrestler and having King Kong Bundy, George ''the Animal'' Steele, and the Motor City Madman all sitting on your chest, one on the other's shoulders like a totem pole. And it smelled considerably better.

''Yaagh,'' Sloan said from the couch next to his. ''Am I still alive?''

He lifted his head and gazed blearily over at McKay. ''*Have* to be," he decided. "If we were dead, there's no *way* we'd be in the same place."

McKay gave him a shit-eating smirk. "Can I help it if I've led a virtuous life?"

Sloan groaned and collapsed back in his couch.

"What are they whining about back there?" Toni Lee asked loudly.

"Oh, they're just not used to pulling gees," Casey replied piously.

McKay shot him the finger, which was wasted because Casey couldn't see it.

Little servomechanized shutters slid open next to the couches, revealing a view of Earth. To McKay it looked surprisingly like egg white just starting to turn color as you stirred it up to make scrambled eggs: not much to see but swirled clouds. It was amazingly bright, even through the polarized port.

"This is one of the amenities the friendly skies of StarVan offers that her competition doesn't," Toni Lee said. "Government designers didn't give shit if the passengers wanted to see out. I just hope none of you gets vertigo."

"Of course not," McKay said, swallowing hard. Another of the criteria they had to meet to get to be Guardians was that they couldn't have vertigo. But there was vertigo and there was vertigo, he decided. This was what you called your extreme kind of case.

Lee unsnapped her harness and floated up off her couch. "Well, we got about thirty minutes before we come out from behind Earth into range of Cygnus."

"I thought we had a couple hours of window left," McKay said.

"We're real high up now, Billy," Casey said. "We're, like, more on their level. Also, we're moving toward them at about twenty thousand klicks an hour."

"Oh."

"You take the wheel, Casey," Lee called, making her way aft to the EVA lock by means of handholds on the couches. "Try not to hot-rod the puppy while I'm outside."

• • •

The famous laser shield was a big disappointment to McKay. It turned out to be a gigantic circular mirror that Toni Lee unfolded and clamped onto the orbiter's snout. Its simplicity was one reason it had been built; planners weren't embarrassed to consider the possibility that a shuttle launch might be attacked by an orbital laser weapon, even if an orbital boarding action was too much for them to swallow.

"What? That's it?" he demanded as she finished the installation. "We brought her along for *that*? It took ten minutes!"

"None of use could've done it that fast, Billy," Tom said. "And we can't afford to make too many mistakes right now."

"That's just mirrorized Mylar, McKay," Sloan said. "It wouldn't be much use to it if you accidentally stuck your foot through it."

"Well, okay, but, I mean, that's *it*? No force fields? No blinky lights? Just a *mirror*?"

"All you need for a laser, Billy," Casey said.

"Right. Go ahead and gang up on me; I can see that it's my day to play class retard—what was that, Navy boy?"

"Nothing, McKay," Sloan said innocently, even though he had quite clearly, if quietly, said, "You got *that* right."

"All right. So how come we can stick this great big disk out front? Won't it slow us down or make it hard to maneuver or something?"

"No air to push against, remember?" Casey said. "Drag doesn't mean much up here."

"Right. I knew that." He scowled, wishing he could punch somebody. That was his classic remedy for stress. He never had a murmur of heart trouble, and he was convinced that was why.

"So how are we gonna steer, then? We can't see dick."

"McKay," said Toni Lee, emerging from the lock area, "we could be sealed in a big tin can with no controls—not to draw any invidious parallels with the early astronauts or anything—and wind up within about a meter of where we intended to be. Cygnus can't maneuver, so it's just a problem in celestial mechanics. And while the Mylar is coated to reflect the whole damn visible spectrum plus a big chunk of both ends, it's radar-transparent, which means we can make any corrections we need to on final approach. Plus we can jettison the shield when we get too close for the laser to bear and need to dock, or at least come to a stop relative to the satellite. Satisfied?''

"No. But I can tell I better shut up so I don't look like a total dummy.''

"You got that right.'' She checked her watch. "Better get your helmets on and your oxygen hoses connected. Don't want you getting the bends, and you're going to run through a real short prebreathing routine as it is.''

The four Guardians were wearing old-fashioned shuttle suits that took 4.3 psi of pressure. The StarVan and Cygnus were pressurized to 14.7 pounds per square inch of oxygen/nitrogen mix. Unless you got as much of the nitrogen flushed from your system before making the transition, you got those painful and possibly fatal little nitrogen bubbles in your bloodstream that divers called the bends.

The orbiter was carrying a modern aluminum-shelled hardsuit specially made for Toni—they weren't the sort of thing you could just take a few tucks in here and there and one-size-fits-all. It carried enough pressure that you didn't risk the bends. But the older soft suits were easier to maneuver in, and also, Vandenberg had some that would fit all the Guardians.

The laser attack came not fifteen minutes after Toni got back inside. That did make McKay reluctantly happy that they'd brought the little bitch. Otherwise it was an even bigger bust than the shield.

"All right, boys,'' the ex-Navy flier called from her couch. "Sensors say we're getting a lot of energy illuminating our shield. Yep, there, they've lit the bastard up.''

McKay craned eagerly out the window—or as eagerly as he could with his helmet on, a necessary part of the prebreathing ritual.

"Where? I don't see anything.''

"You won't, Billy,'' Casey said. "It's a red beam, but

there's no dust up here for it to reflect off of, and no air to ionize."

"What? *What?* I'm being attacked by a real live death ray in outer space and *I can't see anything*?" It was almost too much to take.

"If we didn't have the mirror," Lee said, "you wouldn't see anything, either. Or not for long, if you know what I mean."

McKay did. He decided to sulk, anyway, on general principles. He couldn't wait to reach the station so he could start making people eat shit and die. It had really been one of those weeks.

"We have full power, Dr. Mallory," Sylvie Braestrop said in her singsong Danish lilt that never failed to send a guilty thrill along Mallory's scrotum.

"Nothing is happening, Doctor," Sejnowsky reported from his screen, which showed a digitized image from the orbital-watch telescopes plus an array of other sensors. "Their shield is reflecting over 99.99 percent of our output."

He turned from his console, shock turning his pale face paler. "We will not raise their cabin temperature by five degrees by the time they rendezvous with us."

Mallory looked over his shoulder. Hanging behind him, Hocevar's face was impassive, a hideous tribal mask.

"Your technicians have laid the charges as instructed?" the Hungarian secret policeman asked.

"We've done every little thing you've asked," Mallory said, his light tone not quite concealing his bitterness.

"Ah. Then prepare to initiate self-destruct sequence at my command."

"Ah, you don't think your brave boys will suffice to repel boarders? There are fifteen of them, and four Guardians when last I counted."

"It is well to prepare for every contingency," Hocevar said, and he turned to make for the hardsuit lockers.

Ah, and that's true, you bloody little heathen, Mallory thought after his back. *And I've prepared in ways your little mind cannot even conceive.*

CHAPTER
TWENTY-FOUR ─────────

"Right," Toni Lee's voice crackled in their headsets. *"It's party time."*

Radio-actuated clamps on the mirror array let go of the orbiter's nose. It fell silently aside, propelled by puffs of compressed air from tiny bottles mounted on its frame. The station lay right in front of the StarVan, forty meters dwindling to thirty as Lee completed braking with the maneuvering jets.

"Christ," Billy McKay said. "It looks even more like a big Habitrail from up here."

It did, too, huge and shiny and convoluted in the glare of the naked sun. Out of sight on the other side of the orbiter, Cygnus X-1 poured concentrated energy futilely into outer space.

A square of light appeared at the end of a cylindrical jut. Figures in thick-limbed hardsuits spilled out.

The first hardsuit immediately started to tumble away at a random angle, air spewing out through a hole that had abruptly appeared right in the center of its bulbous chest.

Casey was secured with magnetic clamps and safety lines to the orbiter's nose, firing away with an MP5.

A second figure raised a handgun and fired. He went streaking right straight back into the lock, propelled by the recoil. Braced by the mass of the orbiter, kept stable by the tiny flicks of the maneuvering jets under Toni Lee's exquisitely precise control, Casey shot the third man through the faceplate. He fell back against the hull of the station, spinning slowly.

McKay, Sloan, and Rogers shot little spring-loaded magnetic grapples against the station's hull. "Gently, *dammit*," Lee reminded them as they tugged on the lines to launch themselves toward the station. *"If you pull too hard, you'll make a hell of a hole."*

McKay's guts didn't buy that he'd pulled hard enough, but Casey, Sloan, and Lee had filled his head with enough lurid warnings of what would happen if he tugged too vigorously that he kept from taking another yank. Up here there was no friction to slow them before they hit; as it was, they were to use the little hand-unit propulsion jets they held in their right hands to brake before they hit.

He didn't even want to *think* what he held in his left hand. It was too embarrassing, and he couldn't believe he'd let himself be talked into it. He tucked himself into a ball, used his stomach muscles to orient himself so he was heading feetfirst for the station. His buddies did likewise.

The third hardsuited defender got himself sorted out, braced himself with a hand on the lock frame, started trying to pop out and fire shots from cover. The problem was, his arm had to take the full inertia of his body every time he back-and-forthed. His aim was off, and by his third shot Casey had timed him and split open the side of his helmet. A puff of white water vapor gushed away from his head and he fell back inside.

The lock closed. They must have had some kind of emergency slam cycle, because almost at once it popped open again, emitting a cloud of condensation and four suited figures.

By this time the three Guardians had almost reached the

curved hull of the satellite, and were braking for landing with
brief little licks of gas. They were fouling Casey's aim, so he
let his machine pistol go and shot his own grapple across.

Suddenly the gift of short-swords with half-meter blades—
provided courtesy of Sacker's contacts in the California
SCA—that Scooter, Skids, and Killer had given them didn't
seem so goddam silly.

Toni Lee had lectured them on Weapons in Space. "Guns
are a pain," she said. "Stuff like lubricant tends to evapo-
rate in no time at all, and the quick temperature changes
crystallize the metal in springs and things. You can't count
on too many shots out of them, and there's always the recoil
problem. And once you get inside, you have to use soft lead
ammo unless you want to blow a hole in the hull and let space
in. A good blade will not give you those problems."

And now Billy McKay realized how right she was. The
four men in hardsuits were right out among them, twisting
and trying to bring their handguns to bear.

One had jumped a little too enthusiastically in his eagerness to clear the lock. He streaked right past McKay, hauling
frantically at the lifeline trailing behind him, trying to stop
himself and get back into the fight. Without really thinking
about it, McKay took a hack at the line. He went tumbling
end over end, but the line parted.

Say, that's it for him, isn't it? he thought, watching the
man pinwheel frantically off into the black. *Damn, that's just
neat.*

The other three were too close to Tom and Sloan to shoot,
for fear of hitting each other. The short-swords had no such
difficulty.

Sam let out a rebel yell and drove his full force into the
breastplate of an enormous man whose face was hidden completely by the heavily filtered faceplate. The thin aluminum
shell offered virtually no resistance. The blade buried itself
in the man's sternum and stuck fast.

"Oops," Sloan said as the man's mass twisted the blade
from his hand as he fell away.

More tactically minded, Rogers simply slashed open an
arm of one defender's suit with a single swipe of his sword.

Whether the hardsuit could pinch off airflow to the arm and maintain integrity in the rest didn't matter; no self-sealing process was going to close a twenty-centimeter cut anytime soon, and meanwhile, the man in the suit had a lot of things to occupy his time other than pestering Guardians.

The last man dived back into the lock and started firing blind, frantic rounds out as Casey touched lightly down in a perfect landing.

"Belay me," Rogers said to him and Sloan. They braced themselves with magnetic soles on the hull and took hold of his line as McKay busily reeled himself back to the station.

Tom waited until the firefly-on-angel-dust flicker of the defender's pistol quit. Then he threw himself in front of the lock and fired three quick blasts from the Franchi autoloading combat shotgun he'd unslung. He went rocketing away from the station.

He grunted as he hit the end of the tether. The grapples held, though Sam and Casey came off their feet. As they were all hauling themselves back to the hull, McKay sheathed his sword, unshipped his own Franchi, and went into the lock.

He looked frantically for the controls, which weren't easy to locate. It looked like a compressor loaded with red paint had blown up in here. His buddies crowded into the lock, and Casey palm-stroked a big plate labeled CYCLE IN.

"Oh," McKay said as the outer hatch sealed.

"Company inside, Billy," Tom said, nodding at the thick port that gave into the compartment on the other side.

McKay peered in. Aside from what looked like a bunch of Michelin Tire Men lined along the walls—empty hardsuits— there were four men in black inside, two standing, two kneeling, aiming stubby black pistols at the lock.

Tom's gauntleted hand held up a stun grenade. McKay grinned and nodded. These bad guys weren't suited up— which meant they didn't have face masks polarized to defeat glare.

As the inner hatch began to cycle open, Tom tossed the grenade through the widening crack. Reflexively the four defenders moved to track it. It flashed off right in their faces.

The Guardians had gone flat in a big puppy pile. From the front, McKay and Sloan cut loose with their shotguns. Recoil rammed their boot soles painfully against the sealed outer hatch. It was nothing to what the shots did to the defenders.

Casey and Tom moved to cover the open hatchway that led into the satellite's interior as McKay and Rogers removed their helmets. "Whew, guns sure do make a *mess* in space. Juice everywhere!"

"Splashes propagate spherically out here, Billy," Casey explained earnestly.

"I think that's about all I want to know about it, thank you." He made sure his helmet was hanging properly at the back of his neck and reached for his shotgun, floating conveniently near to hand.

A figure all in black bounced off the wall outside the open hatchway and came hurtling through. It struck McKay in the middle of the chest, and they both flew backward in the open lock.

"Son of a *bitch*," McKay grunted. The man was smaller than he was by a head and a good fifty pounds, but the wiry strength in the arm trying to drive the needle-sharp commando dagger into McKay's neck was incredible. McKay had taken a bad crack on the back of the head, and the lock was showing an alarming tendency to rotate around him, but he hung in there.

They rolled around like fighting cats, tumbling madly in all three dimensions, McKay with one hand locked on his assailant's wrist and the other on his throat. Unable to brace against anything, McKay couldn't use the superior leverage his greater reach gave him, but gradually his mass and brute strength told. The knife receded from his throat and the other man's face began to turn black.

The man brought a knee up sharply into McKay's groin. McKay found out one big disadvantage to the soft suits.

For a moment the strength went out of his entire body. He just managed a feeble, last-half-second push with his left hand, which meant the dagger just laid open the skin on the side of his neck beneath the little shower-cap thingies they all wore to keep their hair from getting in the ventilation system, without slicing open anything too vital.

"Arrgh," McKay said. It was all he *could* say. But his strength came back strong in a wash of fury. He threw the man away from him with all his might, smashed a fist into his face as they rebounded off the walls and into each other again. The back of the man's head slammed hullmetal.

McKay grabbed the rim of the open hatch, pulled himself out. His opponent shook himself and gathered himself for a lunge.

McKay slammed the hatch in his face and hit the CYCLE button.

For a moment the face was pressed against the port, stretched wide open in a scream of fear and fury. A black velvet backdrop appeared behind it. For a millisecond McKay thought he could see dull crimson bloom in the face as capillaries burst beneath the skin. Then the face was gone.

"Ugly motherfucker," McKay said, recovering his helmet, which had gotten knocked adrift but looked intact, and his black bullpup shotgun. "Looked just like one of them Easter Island heads, y'know? Let's boogie on out of here."

They split up outside the suit locker, McKay and Sloan heading right, Rogers and Wilson left. Both routes led to the control compartment. Once they secured it, they could sort things out more or less at their leisure.

The tubular passageways were deserted as they pulled themselves along, which was no big surprise. They didn't know just how much opposition to expect: their files said Cygnus could accommodate fifty at a pinch, but the odds were good there weren't many more than half that inboard. And a lot of them would be technical types, which meant that the Guardians had already more than likely greased most of the enemy's fighting force.

Still, McKay was taking nothing for granted. When a figure popped out of a cross passage right ahead of him, he triggered a blast as Sloan's shouted warning was bouncing around his eardrums.

The recoil fired him back down the passage like a pinball

down a chute. He cursed and bounced helplessly until he collided with Sloan, who managed to stop him at the cost of an clbow in his cyc.

"Sorry," McKay said. "I'll hold on with one hand next time."

His target was hanging in the passage ahead. His rib cage was smashed open and he was as dead as the Watusi. It was a round-headed little Indian looking guy in coveralls that used to be powder blue.

"Oh, no," Sloan breathed. "It was just a scientist. A noncombatant."

McKay remembered other noncombatants—like the children of Vandenberg, not so lucky as Ginny and her Fluffy, whose charred little remains he'd helped pull out of the collapsed buildings three days ago.

"Fuck it," he said. "No noncombatants out here. Come on."

Via communicator, Casey and Tom reported flushing a pair of security men in black jumpsuits, one of whom they killed; the other escaped. The four entered the control room from both ends at the same moment.

A small man with snow-white hair and a blond woman with a pageboy bob and prodigious hooters floated alone in the middle of it. The man smiled and nodded.

"I am Dr. John Mallory," he said, seemingly unfazed by the four black shotgun barrels trained on him. "You must be the Guardians. It's an honor to make your acquaintance."

"Cut the shit," McKay rasped. "What's going on here?"

"Why, nothing," Mallory said with a smile and a lot of Irish. "Except that the station's to blow up in a mere four hundred seconds."

CHAPTER
TWENTY-FIVE ——————

The Guardians looked at each other.

"*Unless,* of course," the scientist went on, "we can come to some kind of accommodation."

"We don't deal with terrorists," McKay said.

"I think you do. I think you have orders to recover this station intact if at all possible."

Sam Sloan bit his lip and looked at McKay. McKay scowled. This was a hell of a note.

"What's going on?" asked Toni Lee's voice in the back of his skull. She was monitoring what went on in the station via mikes clipped to the outsides of the Guardians' softsuits.

"I think you're a man who understands power, Lieutenant . . . McKay, is it?" Mallory tugged gently on the bungee run across the center of the compartment and floated toward a console. "I wonder if you've contemplated how much power a station such as this can offer you."

He stopped himself with the heel of his hand on a padded surface. "The power to make the world over as one desires," he said. "The power to make things *right.*"

"Can you stop the destruct sequence?" McKay asked harshly.

"Sure and I can. It's simple enough. I begin like this—just to display my good faith."

He tapped a sequence on the keyboard. Confidently he glanced down—and the smile slid right off his leprechaun face.

"Wait! Wait just a minute now, that's not the response I'm looking for. What's this? What's all this?"

His fingers flew across the keyboard. He didn't seem to much like the response they were getting.

"Is something wrong, Doctor?" Sloan asked in his best neutral crisis-manager voice.

A shot crashed. Mallory's right shoulder exploded in red. He spun like a top, clutching the wound and gasping in agony.

Sylvie Braestrop had her back against the LCD flatscreen set into the bulkhead, and a snubby pistol—a revolver, like the ones Security used—in both hands. She was well positioned to cover the room.

Casey grabbed Mallory by his uninjured arm and stopped the spinning. Mallory stared at her, his face a ghastly bluish green.

"Why, Sylvie, my love, what is it you've done?"

"I've sabotaged your override sequence. Self-destruct cannot be interrupted—not that I am willing to let you try, for I know how clever you are."

Mallory gaped. *"You getting this, Lee?"* McKay subvocalized.

"Affirmative. Your shit is definitely weak. Give me a minute."

"We don't have a minute."

"But, Sylvie," Mallory choked, "why?"

A tear ballooned out of Sylvie's eye and drifted sadly away. "I love you, John. I love you for your genius, and even more for your vision."

"Five minutes," Sloan remarked conversationally.

The woman twitched the gun at him. He raised his hands and looked so comically inoffensive that McKay figured *he'd* have shot him. But she could barely stand to keep her eyes off Mallory.

"But I also knew that you were weak, John. A woman can tell that about a man."

"These are some crazy fuckers," McKay subvocalized.

"Indeed," Sloan agreed.

"You let Maximov manipulate you, and Hocevar intimidate you," Braestrop said. "I knew that if things went wrong you would equivocate, would try to negotiate."

"But don't you *see,* my love? This offers us another chance—a chance to achieve all we've worked for, suffered for . . . prayed for."

She shook her head. "No, John. It offers you another chance at self-deception. You'd let the Americans string you along as Maximov did, let them take control of our poor Earth for their own ends while you consoled yourself that all you needed was the chance to *act,* and then the power would be yours, to bring about your dream—our dream.

"But I won't let you betray that dream, John. Nor yourself."

"Where is she?" the voice said in McKay's skull.

"What?" he responded, startled into speaking aloud. Neither Mallory nor Braestrop paid him any attention.

"You didn't think I was sitting there at the controls reading Reader's Digest *while you had all the fun? As soon as Casey shoved off I went back and suited up. Now I'm on the outside of the control module."*

"Jesus."

"So where is she, dammit?"

"Now, Sylvie, my dearest dear, let's not be overly hasty," Mallory said. "There's no need for us to destroy ourselves. Put the gun down and we'll be off in the shuttle these gentlemen were thoughtful enough to bring along with them—"

"She's up against the hull," McKay subvocalized.

"Where, you idiot?"

He strained for some identifying feature. *"How the fuck do I know? She's got her back to a screen."*

Sylvie Braestrop was moving her head from side to side,

as if Mallory's words were raindrops and she was trying to shake them off. "It's too late, John. We have failed."

"Which *screen*, McKay? *I know the layout of the control room by heart. I used to fantasize about serving in this station, like some women fantasized about fucking Mel Gibson.*"

Braestrop smiled. "We shall die together, John. You and I, united forever. And we shall die knowing we take with us emissaries of the great evil imperialist power—"

"Hey!" said Casey in outrage.

"*There's a fire extinguisher to the lower left of it, and some kind of hose dingus just to the right.*"

"*Good. It's an emergency oxygen line. Now, where is she, exactly?*"

"*Uh, right side of the screen. My right.*"

"*Your back's to the main console?*"

"*Yeah. I'm just to the right of it.*"

"*Got it. Everybody stand clear.*"

The other Guardians had been following the conversation, unspeaking for fear of confusing the situation somehow—though from their perspective it could hardly have been more confusing. They looked now at McKay.

He shrugged.

"In just"—Braestrop tilted her left arm to check her watch—"four short minutes it will be over, John. I'm sorry I shot you, so very sorry." She was starting to blubber now. "One of you men help him, please, God, it isn't right that his last minutes should be spent in sufferi—"

A perfect red circle appeared under her right breast. A thin scarlet jet sprayed into the center of the compartment, diffusing reluctantly in the swirling currents of the air-circulation system. Her body tilted forward briefly, then slammed back against the bulkhead screen. A hideous sucking sound filled the control room.

The pistol drifted from her hand. She braced her palms against the bulkhead behind her, straining frantically, futilely.

She raised her head and screamed as the merciless vacuum of space sucked her life out through the tiny round hole in the hull behind her.

McKay stared down at the hole in Mallory's main console.

"How'd I do?" Lee asked. *"We need another round?"*

"I don't think so," Sloan said in a hollow voice.

"I knew my old Magnum and a few jacketed loads would come in handy," the aviator exulted. *"You never know when you might want to punch through a space station's hull."*

The passageway outside the control room was clotted with technicians in pastel jumpsuits.

"Clear the fucking way," McKay growled.

One man thrust himself forward. "We demand to be taken with you," he began in a German accent.

McKay shot him through the stomach.

He slammed back into several of his comrades, hosing them with blood. McKay got his feet under him before he hit the far side of the control room, took the shock with his knees. *I'm getting the hang of this shit,* he thought.

He pushed back to the open hatch. "Let's try this again: get out of the way or get blown aside."

They dragged themselves hand over hand down the passageways as fast as they could move, not minding knees and elbows and even heads that got banged in the process. The whole mob of scientific types trooped after them to the suit locker with Mallory at their head, clamoring, pleading—but carefully not demanding.

At the lock, the Guardians paused, Billy and Sam covering the crowd and keeping them at bay outside the suit locker while the other two put on their helmets. Then Casey split out the lock while Tom took over standing off the Cygnus people. Toni Lee would never get out of her hardsuit in time to get them clear of the station before the charges blew.

Mallory thrust himself into the locker as McKay dogged his helmet. "Please," he gasped. "You've got to help us. You can't just abandon us to die here. For the love of God—"

McKay's gloved hand caught him by the throat. " 'God,' " McKay growled. "Interesting choice of words. You fuckers here were all set up to play God from orbit, weren't you, lording it over all the rest of us measly insects?"

Mallory was shaking his head in speechless denial. "McKay, come *on!*" Sloan yelled from the lock.

"So if you're *gods*," McKay yelled, "fucking *walk* home!"

He threw Mallory into the panic-stricken faces of his followers and stepped into the lock. It closed behind him and instantly evacuated its contents into space.

Floating out, McKay gave the doomed technicians the finger. Then he turned, grabbed the line Casey had left strung between the shuttle and the station, and kicked off.

Sloan grabbed McKay by the arm and reeled him into the lock. "Everybody aboard!" he shouted over the communicators as he dogged the lock's outer hatch.

McKay felt instant acceleration. He beat his fist impatiently against the bulkhead while oxygen hissed endlessly into the little chamber.

At last the door swung open. "Home free!" McKay crowed, popping his helmet open.

And then he was tumbling heels over head, and the lights went where they go when they go out.

EPILOGUE ———————————————

"What the fuck?" McKay *sputtered when he got most of his senses back.*

The first thing he got in focus was Sloan's face, hovering centimeters above his. "Well, at least I know I ain't dead—" *he began.*

"Okay, okay, McKay, nobody likes a sore winner."

"What happened?"

"We caught a chunk of debris from the station, Billy," Casey *explained from the pilot's couch. "But we're okay."*

"Well," Sloan *said skeptically, "if by 'okay' you mean we lost one of our engines and most of our attitude jets, and are going to crash in Alaska."*

"Land, Sam," Casey *said aggrievedly. "I can get us down in one piece."*

"Swell," McKay *said.*

"Any landing you can walk away from is a good landing."

"I might also add for the record," Toni Lee *said from the next couch, "that the heroine of the moment received a busted port wing as her reward for saving your male chauvinist ba-*

con, McKay. I'll now gladly accept the plaudits of the grateful multitude."

"Yeah," McKay grunted. "Thanks. You don't shoot too
bad for a broad."

"Cocksucker. When I get a cast on this arm, I'm going to
bust your nose with it."

"Go right ahead. My day's already shot."

"But what's your gripe, McKay? We won, and we all survived. Isn't that victory?"

"Yeah. Even if we didn't get President Jeff his laser back,
we did win.

"But we're going to crash-land—is that okay with you,
Case?—crash-land in Alaska, and it's cold in Alaska, and
last I heard there were commies in Alaska."

He let the bitching run down and stared out the viewport.
There was the Earth, coming right at them.

"You know," he said, "I don't think I'm ever gonna leave
the ground again."